Some jobs are worth dying for...

I did *not* sign up for this. I did not exactly sign up for any of it, to be truthful, but I did have a choice. I could have found another job somewhere. In some part of the world, there would have been someone who would see a novelist as an asset instead of a security risk. I remembered sitting across from that human slug Wanda Laird, and how she made me feel like a bug she wanted to squish, and tried to make me think she would ruin me if I refused.

But I also remembered thinking about what my name would look like in the history books. How it would be my account you all would read. My voice that would give narrative cohesion to the dry collection of logs. My observations that would give substance to the characters.

No sane, intelligent person would refuse. I came because I wanted to.

As storm clouds gathered in the valley below me, I wished I had found the courage to admit that to myself before I came. It might have made a difference, somehow.

It was supposed to be a heroic tale, like the *Ramayana*. I was Valmiki, bringing the great tale to all who came after. If I knew it was going to turn out this way, if I even thought it was possible, I might not have come.

Also by J. Daniel Sawyer

The Antithesis Progression
Predestination
Free Will
Avarice (coming 2015)

The Clarke Lantham Mysteries
And Then She Was Gone
A Ghostly Christmas Present
Smoke Rings
Silent Victor
He Ain't Heavy

Standalone Works
Down From Ten
Ideas, Inc.
Suave Rob's Double-X Derring-Do

Nonfiction
Making Tracks: A Writer's Guide to Producing Audiobooks
Science Fiction Weaponry: A Guide for Writers (with Mary Mason)
Throwing Lead: A Writer's Guide to Firearms and the People Who Use Them (with Mary Mason)

Collections
Sculpting God: Bedtime Stories for Adults
Frock Coat Dreams: Romances, Nightmares, and Fancies from the Steampunk Fringe
Tales of a Lombard Alchemist, Volume 1 (forthcoming)

THE
RESURRECTION
JUNKET

J. DANIEL SAWYER

AWP Science Fiction
A division of AWP Books

ISBN-13: 978-0-9915458-1-0
ISBN-10: 0-9915458-1-8

Book Design by ArtisticWhispers
Cover Art "Planet Filbert" © 2015 by J. Daniel Sawyer and Kitty
NicIaian

www.artisticwhispers.com

DEDICATION

I wrote this for you, the reader, in honor of the infinite horizon before us
May humanity continue to hold her nerve.

What a piece of work is a man, how noble in reason, how infinite in faculties, in form and moving how express and admirable, in action how like an angel, in apprehension how like a god! the beauty of the world, the paragon of animals—and yet, to me, what is this quintessence of dust?
-William Shakespeare, Hamlet Act 2, Scene 2

All life is code.
-Juan Enriquez

Consequence

It used to be a bright city, lit with a hundred billion little lights. Each one a signal.
A thought.
A feeling.
An impulse.
A physical instantiation of meaning.

Then, more quickly than she might have expected, the lights winked out. When the last axon failed to respond to the last electrochemical impulse flowing over the last synapse from the last dendrite, the city went dark.

And Xiyi died.

Chapter 1

A New Vantage

Introduction
Expedition: Filbert
Mission Historian Personal Perspective
Mission Day 30
Year 2253 of the Common Era

I, CHAN XIYI AYA, am number thirty-six.

That should be a nice round number. It is not. Thirty-six is the number of exclusion. It marks me out as the one who does not really belong.

Eight weeks ago, I emerged from quarantine. Last in line for awakening means last in line for release—they have to prod your immune system so it can handle the native hazards, at least the ones that they know about. Growing the super-Ts, then testing them, is said to take some time. We were warned, but hearing about a thing and doing a thing are not the same. By the time I saw the sky, the rest had already sorted out the living situation, divvied up the responsibilities, implemented the initial organization of the expedition. As the official tag-along, I do not get a voice. Given everything else, I prefer it that way.

My title is "Official Civilian Observer, Expedition: Filbert." It is not exactly a military expedition, but the word "Civilian" fits. The Americans have a saying about "Jack of all trades, master of none." Well, you play a lot of cards sitting around in quarantine, and within two days of my release, I put together that I am more of a "three of all trades" who might make Jack if she sticks with this project for the next twenty years or so, and doesn't go spare from boredom.

The mission gods planned it that way, of course. That is what a Civilian Observer is supposed to do. I am a sort-of quality control measure, in beta-test form. This round of missions is the first time they have used people like me, in various quantities. Me, here, on this mission? I am the only one. Lucky me. The theory is that we designated idiots will spot problems that all the specialists and the commander do not notice.

Filbert is the name they picked for our fair planet. Someone in the home office determined that a playful and stupid planet name would make the job feel less daunting for the sorts of people they send out.

I am not sure how the other teams decided to organize their quarantine period, so here's how we did ours. The commander—Dr. Darren Galbraith—was the first to get released into our ground station, and from there he decided in what order everyone else should come out. Since he did not find anything amiss that might need specialized attention, he chose to bring people out in order of authority. Department heads first, then the research scientists, then the physical plant team, then me. By the time I saw my first glimpse of sky, the colony was fully functional, and I had a duty roster.

They made me the designated floater. When the waste team needs an extra pair of hands to perform a task they haven't yet built a robot for, they call me. And when I'm not doing the work of a *dalit*, I spend my time looking over shoulders, asking questions, trying to understand what everyone is doing.

Most of that data will not make it into these journal reports, but I need to understand it much better than I do at present, if I am to make anything useful out of myself. Being useful is not an easy thing to do when you are stuck in the middle of a quarantine zone on an uninhabited planet, surrounded to suffocation by the thirty-five most boring people Earth had to offer.

Perhaps "boring" is not fair. "Emotionally stable" is what they selected for. But it *is* boring. And old. They all have well-maintained bodies, just like anyone else, but youth is just a cellular matter. Age, the sort that matters, seeps into the soul. I am the youngest person on this planet by at least fifty years, and every conversation I have reminds me that I am little more than a schoolgirl sitting at the adults' table at a wedding feast. I never felt so out of place, not even at school. Now, as I did then, I spend my free moments walking outside, trying to locate myself in the world I can only see through the plasma fences that keep out the local flora and fauna.

They also keep us, the visitors, in. Our own human zoo. The animals that come to visit, attracted by the field—the small ones come right up to the fence, but sometimes we see the larger ones hiding back, just behind the flora, watching us. We cannot see them so well, cannot classify them. But what we can see, and what our probes show us, give us a body plan for their chordate animals. They have backbones, or something that serves the same purpose straight down the middle, with segmented strutted rib cages, and organs and muscles positioned all around the body in a spiral pattern, making their necks and backs less vulnerable go breakage and changing the dynamics of everything they do. I trust that Dr. Sansa will forgive me if I have made any errors of terminology.

But we go to the fence to see them. I go every day. And they come, drawn by the electrical fields, and they see us, trapped inside. Us, and all our pathogens and botanicals. For safety, ours and theirs whatever lurks out there beyond what we can see through the brush.

The mission gods—I assume it was the mission gods—chose for our home base a marvelous vista. The compound was built by the robots between the landing and the end of our quarantine. We were not conscious for most of it. They have located us on a high hill, backed up to a sheer cliff. They burned down to bare dirt the hilltop around us, sterilized it, and cultivated it for Earth-type vegetation. We need to be able to live safely and in biological isolation until the team finishes phase one, and has the data to make its decisions about our integration plan.

Expedition: Filbert
Mission Day 43
Mission Historian Personal Perspective
Year 2253 of the Common Era

Up until this morning, things were going as well as could be expected, operationally speaking—which is the reason it has taken me this long to put together my first proper entry. Everything has progressed by the numbers, according to the schedule they laid out back home, so I have not had much to report.

This afternoon, after rotating the agar plates in the culture lab, I walked the perimeter. Inside the boundary are the five domes and the small farm. Outside, dense forest stretches its amethyst fingers up from the valley's broad floor, gripping the hills like a prize. Between them, a broad river of phosphor-rich water snakes its way down into a spectacular canyon stretching all the way to the horizon. At night, it glows faintly, like a glow worm. The canyon is surrounded by high plateaus furred with vegetation that, like the forests, tends toward the purple, with bright green and yellow splashes here and there.

We have not yet seen any flying creatures. The first time I asked about the lack of birds, Dr. Sansa—Christiana—gave me a forty minute lecture on cladistics, over breakfast. Never again will I dare utter aloud that word in connection to this planet's flora.

"Birds are impossible here," she'd said. "The entire notion of 'bird' presupposes an evolutionary history concomitant with...okay, look. It's like calling bats 'birds' because they fly, even though they're mammals. Trust me on this one. It doesn't come from Earth's evolutionary tree, it's not a bird, ipso facto. If we found flying animals here, they'd be 'avian life forms', maybe. Flying creatures, that is fine too. But birds? Not a chance."

Now, I really love Christiana. She is so sweet, so caring, you will never find a better person in any five planets. But after forty minutes of that I was ready to put a dozen eggs under her sheets so I could hear her scream when she got into bed.

But at least I can say it here, since they all think what I do is some kind of pulp fiction enterprise. Birds birds birds birds. Whatever you want to call them, they do not exist here, at least not on this part of the planet. Nearest they come are enormous flying bugs about as wide as a large man's hand.

Bugs. That's another cladistic mistake, I'm sure. Christiana, if you ever read this, think of those eggs, and hold your tongue. I'm trusting you with this.

So, walking. Yes. Along the fence. The view has yet to bore me. The afternoon sun shot through the hazy atmosphere, broken up by the clouds, like laser spears from our orbiting base station. They ignited little blooms of bright color, which burst out from the surrounding deep purple like bunches of overripe berries. I wish I could say it would always look that way, but I can't. We might have to change it, and then this, and the images and videos and holos stored with it, will be the only record.

I hope we do not have to change it.

As I walked, one of the robotics technicians —Lundi—flagged me from the main building, where we keep the assembly hall and the mess. Histology had an urgent announcement.

Tomorrow was supposed to be our first day for preliminary departmental reports, so an announcement from Histology was not unexpected. Their first round of experiments was a sample catalog of the local floral and fauna, evaluating them for suitability for cultivation and domestication. The more that humans can do in-situ, the better the news for the civilization that the colonists will eventually build here.

The early urgency must mean something exciting, I thought, which suited me quite well, as I have been going out of my mind with boredom—which, come to think of it, is another topic that I need to do a report on. The Foundation has some serious re-thinking to do with the way it selects and manages its personnel.

Dr. Prescott—he has asked me to call him Hal, but he is not my friend, and is seventy years older than I am, has five doctorates, and left his great grandchildren behind to join this junket—plodded into the mess and did not bother to take a seat:

"Ladies and gentlemen, I've got the results back on the protein analysis from the first swath of the native biome. Not to put too fine a point on it, but we are officially screwed."

When he said that, my stomach dropped into my pelvis.

He went on to explain that there seemed to be a quirk in the local evolution that happened early in the planet's history that rendered everything he had analyzed unfit for human consumption. Maybe even unfit for human contact. He said: "It's chemical warfare on an apocalyptic scale."

Nobody said this would be an easy job, but they are now trying to decide whether it is even possible to make this place suitable for human habitation. It may not be worth the attempt.

Reflection

Dying wasn't so bad, she decided, once you got used to it.

Granted, it wasn't the world's most entertaining hobby. Frankly, it hurt like hell. The delirium had its good points, though. Not that she'd remember much of it. That was the point of being dead, after all. When your brain stops working, not a lot of thinking goes on—or if it does, there's no way to remember it.

Is there a difference between thinking something and forgetting it, and never thinking it in the first place?

If an axon fires and no dendrite feels it, does it make a thought?

Chapter 2

The Program

WANDA LAIRD'S OFFICE AT the San Diego facility was as bellicose and ostentatious as the woman herself. A sharp-eyed bat who had arrested her aging in her early fifties, and as big around the middle as she was tall, she did not manage to conceal the cruel smirk behind her diplomatic grin. Not that she really tried.

She sat behind an old, grizzled wooden desk, filled with knots and twists, sanded and polished to a mirror sheen. It was the kind of desk good only for intimidating underlings like Xiyi. Under Laird's withering gaze, she felt even smaller than the one hundred fifty-five centimeter frame bequeathed to her by her Himalayan ancestors.

Xiyi, who at this point had not yet experienced the dubious pleasure of her own death, took careful notes, determined to put a parody of Dr. Laird into her next book as revenge for forcing her through this tiresome meeting when she could have spent the afternoon not-working on greeting the non-existent visitors that theoretically might materialize outside the Foundation's front doors.

"It *is* quite a promotion, Ms. Chan." It wasn't the words, so much, as the tone that sounded a warning in the pit of Xiyi's stomach. If ever there was a person regarding whom "human" was a useless adjective, it was Laird. That was what made her a good department head, and it was a quality that Xiyi had always respected. Until now.

"And you are offering this to me? Why?" Sitting in the beam of that clinical gaze made her feel like a specimen being readied for dissection. "I am no planetary scientist. You have people here who have worked eighty years just for this chance, and you wish to send me?"

"It has come to our attention," the head's corpulent frame leaned toward Xiyi, looming over her without ever stirring from her quasi-throne, "that you've carved out quite a name for yourself in the fiction world. Not an easy game these days. Not exactly reputable."

Xiyi became—though she'd not have believed it possible—even more acutely aware of her minute stature, but she kept her voice level, without a hint of a quaver. "My time is my own. My stories are my business."

"And when your stories include confidential information that you obtained through abusing your position? When they feature caricatures of respected businessmen, and hectoring depictions of your coworkers, who come through that door and complain to me about it?"

Xiyi's chair seemed to grow six sizes—just enough to make her feel like a rabbit in a wolf's cage, not enough to let her hide under the cushion.

"You are a drain on this company's resources, a scourge on its morale, and, frankly, an embarrassment to anyone possessing even a modicum of self-respect. We've reviewed the available options. You have a good eye for detail. Almost a journalist's eye. At the moment the pool is made up of specialists in the relevant fields. However, it has been a matter of some concern that the Foundation has never provided for the presence of a biased observer. Someone who might bring out the elements invisible to the data crunchers. They asked us to help create a pool of chroniclers for the experiment. Since we have not yet filled the slate, I've decided to offer you a choice. You may stay here, and we will prosecute you to the fullest extent. Or you may go, and chronicle one of the missions."

"But, why must..."

"This is a long-term experiment. Success means you'll be away for decades. A return ticket means coming back to a world that won't recognize you."

"And if I wanted to..."

Ms. Laird cocked an improbably pointy eyebrow, managing to look rather like a wizened toad affecting vague amusement at the misfortunes of her pollywogs. "If the experiment is a success, you will have every opportunity to travel wherever you want, even back here. Though I doubt very much it's an experience you'll wish to embrace a second time."

Xiyi didn't know what to make of that. She'd never learned the details of the new travel process, but assumed that it must somehow involve cryonics, which had a nasty reputation for coma terrors. She frankly wasn't enthused about going through that experience even once.

THE FIRST SERIES OF CLASSES in the indoctrination program (they called them "cycles," for reasons which escaped Xiyi) had laid her groundwork in the scientific background she would need to establish even a basic understanding of the mission, and flew by easier than she—an artist by temperament and education—had expected. A few months after her uncomfortable encounter with the Laird of the Slugs, she found herself sitting in her second cycle classes as if she were a freshman all over again.

The Marathon Planetary Foundation had learned through long experience that, for their purposes, the most effective method of indoctrination was the Socratic workshop. Part interactive lecture, part group discussion, it recalled ancient educational traditions long since abandoned. For conveying information, the format was woefully inefficient. But for encouraging evaluation and solidarity, it remained unbeatable, and in the eyes of the Foundation, those were the things that really mattered.

All their low level corporate training was conducted this way. It had the added advantage of allowing the Mission Stability Engineers—or "the gods of the mission," as the candidates referred to them—to spot potential personality conflicts and avoid future trouble.

It had worked since the first successful Mars expedition, and they didn't intend to change their process now, even if they were venturing into novel waters by bringing in the neurotypicals.

The lecturer, George—who, being strictly a mouthpiece and not a group mentor, was not afforded the dignity of a surname—paced the stage idly while performing his well-practiced lesson.

"Today, we start from first principles. All other things being equal, the transmission of information over intrasystem distances is limited to the speed of light. A signal from here to Mars, bounced and boosted through any of the orbital stations, faces a round trip of between eight and forty-eight minutes. With standard packet verification, this means that a single bit of information will take approximately sixteen minutes at opposition. That's your best case."

"But sir," Xiyi shouted out, "I visited Phobos Station when I was twelve years old, and we had no problem with network access delays."

"A clever workaround. Interplanetary mirror nodes sync every day across the solar systems. Redundant Internets, to provide the illusion of quick access. Nothing on a non-local node happens in real-time, as you'll have noticed if you attempted a coms linkup. It all flows over the same network—since text browser access is asynchronous, we can use asynchronous tricks to give people the illusion of real-time access.

"Now, in any network, over vast distances you're confronted with the problem of information verification. The back and forth necessary to recover dropped packets and verify the integrity of the received information eats up a spectacular amount of time. The farther away you get, the more you're subject to the laws of diminishing returns." A giant graph appeared on the screen behind him, plotting ascending astronomical units on the y axis and descending transmission efficiency on the x axis. "Once you pass a certain point—and that point varies according to the nature and amount of the information being transmitted—it becomes faster and more cost-effective to move information storage devices from one place to another. All the verification is done at the point of transmission, so the fidelity is assured at the point of receipt. And, of course, you don't have to worry about interference disrupting the signal along the way. Solar storms and gamma ray bursts don't disrupt shielded media.

"I know this must sound very pedestrian to all of you. I

can hear you asking yourselves 'What? I sold my soul for *this*?'
Well, that's because what I've just explained to you is the entire
basis of our proprietary long range space travel technology."

Xiyi, and the six hundred other members of the
audience—other excursion candidates, trainees, Foundation
folks studying for promotions, donors, and old hats bringing
themselves up to speed with parts of the Foundation's vision
normally invisible from their narrow specialties—collectively
shifted in their seats, as if a small tsunami had just passed
under the floor.

"I must remind you that everything you're hearing in this
session is strictly confidential, and any leaks, even to your
nearest and dearest, will result in prosecution to the fullest
extent. What you're about to hear may disturb you. We're
doing this class the old-fashioned way so that we can deal with
those feelings and ensure that you actually understand what
you're signing up for. Because we're about to turn your world
upside-down."

Another slide appeared behind him that obligingly read:
Everything you think is upside down.

"Everything you understand about the world, from your
day-to-day experience, is wrong. In fact, it's *exactly* wrong. Now,
this isn't going to come as news to most of you. Most of you
know that you're made of atoms, which are mostly composed
of empty space and probability, but you also know that it
doesn't matter at our level. We're not subject to quantum
effects the way a photon is, and that's probably a good thing.
It's a chaotic world down there, after all."

The slide changed to another single line caption: *Matter
Does Not Matter*

"Ever since Socrates, philosophers have debated whether
matter was real or illusory—good, or evil, if you will.

Materialists held that it's all that there is, while Platonists held that it was a corrupting force that debased the noble content of the spirit. You'll find further reading on these in your orientation materials, if you're someone who gets into philosophy. Chapter six is a pretty complete digest, so we won't cover it in depth here. Suffice it to say: good or bad, matter is the basic point of contact between all the different traditions that have, over the millennia, tried to figure out what the hell all of this," he made a sweeping gesture to encompass the entire universe, "is here for.

"But what if..." he paused for emphasis, "what *if*...matter didn't *matter*. Oh, we're still all made out of it. It's still what the accessible part of our universe is made of, but do you think it *really* matters which atoms are in your body, as long as they're in the right proportion? You shouldn't. You're changing out atoms all the time. Your body runs on molecules. The *particular* stuff you're made of matters exactly as much as the *particular* pieces of sand in a sand castle." He paused for a moment, to let the thought sink in, then continued. "It's not the *stuff* you're made of that matters. It's how it's *arranged*."

Another slide: *First Principle*

"The arrangement of matter is information. Information by itself isn't privileged. *Chaos* is information. Even *noise* is information. *Everything* is information, so information is not special. Information is not rare.

"But information *is* king. Who you are, what you think, how you're shaped, none of it is defined by the stuff you're made of—it's all defined by how that stuff is arranged. The essential you, the thing that makes you *you*, is information."

Another slide: *Second Principle*

"Information, any information, can be read. This is axiomatic. If it can't be read by something, it's not information. You all know your DNA, and its expressions and epigenetic inflections, can be read. You all know that your neural map can be read. Anytime you go in for surgery, both get backed up in case there's any mishap.

"This isn't to say it isn't information if *we* can't read it. Science's only job is to reduce our illiteracy."

A hand shot up.

"Yes, Doctor Ansari."

"I believe you'll find the consensus view, as expressed first by Popper, is that science is an error detection mechanism to minimize the possibility of misapprehension..."

"Yes, yes, critical realism." George waved at the air as if swatting flies. "But error detection for what?"

"For the testing of conclusions based upon empirical observations."

"And how does one reach those conclusions?"

"Based upon previous experience."

George looked at the whole audience and shrugged theatrically. "We could go on all day like this, couldn't we? An infinite regress taking us all the way back into the history of science. Thank you, Doctor Ansari. I believe you'll find that what I'm saying is perfectly compatible with Popper."

Doctor Ansari sat down. From where she sat, Xiyi imagined she could distinguish a skeptical scowl on his face.

"You see," George started pacing again, "those empirical observations are meaningless in and of themselves, unless they can be plugged into a theory that gives them meaning. We find the limits of our theories when the meaning we think we've discovered ceases to fit the observations we've accumulated —that would be Kuhn's insight, Doctor Ansari..."

A ripple of uncharitable laughter swept through the room. Ansari's scowl lost what little bit of openness it previously held.

"...and we discover that thanks to the critical realist's toolkit propounded by Popper. But the reason that we're able to construct theories at all is because things truly are systematic in nature. Physics has its own language, which emerges from theory and then becomes independent of theory as it begins to express and critique the theory. Biology is the same. We have learned some of the algorithms—the axioms and grammar, if you will—that comprise nature, through the kind of research you all do here on this very campus. You are, at bottom, linguists of the universe—because each sort of information is written in its own peculiar language.

"The entire object of scientific research is to learn more languages, so we can read more of the information out there.

"But for something to be information, it must, in theory, be readable. Maybe not by us, but at least by *something*. Other atoms, the universe itself, anything else you care to imagine, as long as it exists.

"Information that is not readable is not information. It only becomes information when a system, or a mechanism, exists to read it. This is important, because..."

He summoned the next slide: *Third Principle*

'Space is very big. Even with the Mannix-Alcubierre drive, it can take decades to get to some points even in our corner of the galaxy. This is the reason all our major expeditions have either been generation ships or small satellite space probes. And, as we learned with the Proxima One disaster, coming out of transition can expose everyone to catastrophic doses of radiation if things aren't handled exactly right.

"We've gotten better at it since then, but we've still not sent any major long-range human explorers out past the first perimeter. Mass is still an obstacle, and we've run up against a wall in the laws of physics when it comes to being able to pack enough juice to make those transitions viable. We can send probes, but anything bigger than about four tons can't get beyond the first perimeter.

"But this isn't news to any of you, I'm sure."

Another slide: *Fourth Principle*

"Given the right machinery, information—any information—can be rewritten. Again, not controversial. We've had some pretty publicized cases, starting with the Harrisburg Twins, where we've restored neural maps from backups. Most of you right now have domestic robots with wetware CPUs that were written in at the factory."

Xiyi found herself nodding along. Even she, growing up as a refugee in bases from Morocco to her final stop in Salida at age nineteen, had always had wetware bots around. They were cheaper to maintain than traditional pets, and could be re-tasked for household chores at the push of a button. Everyone had at least one.

"Fifty years ago, we here at The Foundation realized that if you put these principles in the right order, they add up to a novel method of transmitting information over vast distances. We've spent the last five decades perfecting that method, and now, we're ready to deploy it."

The speaker let the room catch up with him. He waited for the collective gasp. When it came, he smiled.

"I think that's enough for the morning session. Go get lunch. The discussion groups will convene back here in two hours."

AFTER THE BREAK, SHE joined her assigned discussion group to hash through all the procedures related to transmitting information over vast distances, including biological information. Even for a highly educated laywoman, the conversation quickly spiraled out of her depth. By the end of the afternoon she felt as if she'd been forced to drink a waterfall. When her head hit the pillow, she entered dreams filled with a melange of words, none of which seemed to fit together.

The next day, they toured some of the facilities, and got to view the vehicles, and her mind got a chance to latch on to tangible things, and connect them to the torrent of words and ideas. The three stages of her fate:

The launch vehicle, squat with engines like flower-petals arrayed around its central fuel tank, with contact rails laid into the surface to give it better grip against the launch catapult's impeller field for its trip out of the atmosphere. Its head, flat and with grappling points, designed to attach to the second stage: The drive-ship.

Bright, polished silver everywhere—long and needle-shaped, about ten meters across, designed to dock to the drive unit already waiting at the construction depot in high orbit, topping off its fuel tanks with antimatter harvested from the Van Allen belts. Xiyi listened to the impressive technical specifications that, thanks to her classwork, she could mostly follow except on the finer theoretical points of field control, and, while she listened, she watched. The skin of the ship seemed to change color and texture as she watched, cycling from bright silver to deep black, from smooth to crenelated to ringed and ridged. The tour guide explained, when he saw Xiyi and several others watching, that the changeable skin allowed for fine-grained control of drive field interactions, and for more efficient energy harvesting, and—for reasons Xiyi did not quite understand—for better navigation.

And then, to fit inside the drive ship, the lander module. Smaller than she would have expected, even considering that most of their equipment would be built on-site by the advanced robot expeditions that were, even now, preparing the ground before them.

Her mind latched on to the shapes, the textures, and paired them with the ideas they represented. They melded in her mind, settling down into her consciousness, sewing in her disquiet and anticipation bundled together as if they were two names for the same feeling.

That night, her dreams were cold and bright, like a serene cleanroom in a cryo facility.

THE INDOCTRINATION PROGRAM was a months-long intensive affair. In the time since she'd been encouraged to enroll, Xiyi had developed a close knot of compatriots. At the center of that knot was Solly, a scrubby-headed Ethiopian boy who could make anybody laugh. Xiyi had found herself secretly hoping that he would be assigned to her mission.

The next day, after meeting with her writing coach to review her previous week's output and get some new exercises, she made her way to the dormitory to see if he was available for a walk around the grounds.

When she knocked on his door, it swung inward to reveal a rumpled bed with a half-packed bag on it.

"Solly? You here?"

His smoked-caramel voice came from the bathroom. "Yeah, be out in a minute."

A flush. A little rush of water in a basin. The door opened and Solly stepped through, half dressed in his business slacks. "Xiyi. Need something?" He gave her a quick little half-smile and pushed past her to the bed, where he resumed stuffing his duffel.

"I thought a walk..what are you doing?"

"Getting out of here."

"What? Why?"

"Have you been around this week? Paying some kind of attention?"

"Yeah, and?"

"They're going to kill us. Well, those of us they pick to go out. And the rest of us are party to murder."

"They didn't say that, they just said...it was about information transfer to outer colonies."

"Including biological information."

"Of course," Xiyi shrugged. "Livestock, cultures, crops..."

"And us. They said we are information. Hell, Xi, weren't you listening at all?" He recapped the mass/distance equation describing the Mannix limit on drive travel. He did a theatrical recap of the four basic principles. "So that's how they get us to that distant star."

"Don't be a puce. They put us in cryo..."

"With those mass limits? Have you done the math yet? They've either got to copy us and send out the copies and leave us normal people to schlep around here, or kill us. I don't know about you, but I don't want a thousand Solly's wandering around the galaxy sharing the same soul, and I sure as hell don't want to die for these wackos. No, no, I intend to live a long time, and when I die I want to go to heaven..."

Xiyi couldn't help rolling her eyes. Even great people like Solly could cling to outdated, boneheaded ideas.

"Oh, no. Don't look at me like that, Ms. 'Reincarnation.'"

She flashed hot. "Asshole."

"Ah, hell. Look, I'm sorry, okay? But look, if you thought...oh never mind. Anyway, this is not for me, not no how. So I'm going home."

"But, your grandmother..."

"There are other ways to get rejuvs. No no no, Xiyi, these bastards aren't gonna nail Solly Abate to the scanning table. They're not gonna kill me or clone me and turn me into some kind of drone slave. No way no how. I'm outta here."

Xiyi didn't have a good answer. She didn't like the idea—didn't fancy not being able to actually experience the trip. She didn't believe in Solly's version of a soul—some single entity wedded to her body, something that might get confused if she changed bodies all at once instead of one piece at a time like everyone else did as they started aging—and the thought of going into microstorage for a spaceflight bothered her less than the notion that they might send a clone and imprint it with one of her neural backups. But nobody did that kind of thing. "Illegal" didn't even begin to cover the seriousness of the offense.

"But they don't do that. It's illegal. They'd shut this place down in a heartbeat and sell all the assets to SystemCorps or some other competitor, right? I mean, remember what they did with The Sigma Five Foundation?

"Xiyi, they're not doing it *here*. They'll do it *out there*. Do you really think the law applies halfway across the galaxy? Who's gonna prosecute it, huh? You think there's some kind of galactic district attorney that's gonna say 'Oh, gee, look at those scofflaws out in the next cluster. Perhaps we ought to bring the civilizing hammer of justice down upon them with the queen's good law.'" His lip twitched in contempt. She caught it, and part of her heart cracked open. Up until that moment, they'd been buds. "They'll do it and they'll get away with it and there's nothing you or I can do about it. You can't be that dumb. Come on, think!"

Xiyi's stomach washed hot with anger, then a dead chill followed as her mind caught up to the full horror of what he was saying. What if they *did* just turn out copies? What if there wound up being dozens of her roaming the cosmos? Would they all dilute her share of spirit? Would her life fade to dull gray?

She didn't want to think about it, and now she was too angry to care anymore that Solly was leaving.

A knock from behind interrupted her brooding.

"Howdy campers!" Xiyi turned to see Dar, one of the second-cyclers on his third PhD, and probably the most bored human being she'd ever met. "Time to roust those bones and get down to the athletic field."

Solly grumbled.

"Oh, don't be like that. We've got naked croquet and mud wrestling scheduled for ten minutes from now, we can just make it."

Solly flipped him off.

"Okay, I lied. But there is food."

Solly didn't come. Xiyi muttered a vague goodbye and accompanied Dar to the buffet-style cookout in the evening air.

The Foundation had decided, in their infinite wisdom, that everyone needed something homey and grounding for the mid-week recreation. If Solly had come with them, the distraction might have worked. He and Dar made great entertainment, and on most evenings she bounced between them like a ping-pong ball in a high-energy verbal game. It kept her language skills sharp and her mind sharper, and when their other friends joined in, things could go on all night.

It didn't seem to matter that she was one of the youngest and least educated people here—everyone was young in body if not in mind, and all were getting their concept of the universe stretched out like a lump of taffy while committing to memory an insane and complicated set of social rules, experimental protocols, and a completely new sense of law and justice, custom designed to help them all survive the years they were about to spend in dangerous environments.

She seemed to belong, and that helped to quell her disquiet.

At least, temporarily.

Regret

The last real memory, the one that happened before her brain started to swirl and bend and slip into the light, was the bullet. It tore through her abdomen, a burning numbness spreading through her body faster than the hot rip of the hollow-point could shred her organs.

She'd chosen that part. A childish obsession with ancient weapons that she never dreamed she'd indulge. Thrill death wasn't exactly her thing. She didn't even like eating synthetic beef—you could never quite tell that some sentient animal hadn't been slipped in on the side, to enhance the taste.

But she had to die. That was her part of the bargain. They did allow her to choose the circumstances of her demise. So she asked to be shot before they put her down. Leave her with one less unanswered question as she faced the long darkness.

Chapter 3

The Colonists' Dilemma

Expedition: Filbert
Mission Day 237
Mission Historian Personal Perspective
Year 2253 of the Common Era

IN ORDER TO EXPLAIN THE events of the past six months, I should give you the definitive recipe for creating a science colony:

Take one team of mission resource specialists, and add a committee of centenarian psychometricians. Put a full slate of AIs at their disposal, and turn the entire mix loose on your pool of candidates. This cabal is what we call "The Mission Gods," since they create the world we have to live in, and, by Byzantine rules of responsibility, we get to find out if it works.

They put the candidates under a microscope, observing all the little interactions. Every facial expression, change of pulse, change of breathing, and stray swallow. They learn everything about everyone, including the things that the candidates don't know about themselves.

Then, they go through their evaluation.

First, they prefer age and expertise—important when entering a challenging environment. They want people with old minds and long memories. Experience is the survival capital of a science colony. They explained it to us at length during indoctrination.

After that, they filter people for stability, since the last thing you want to experience, a hundred light years from nowhere, is a psychotic break. Schizos and borderlines can fool you at coffee, but they can't fool the brain scan. Neither can psychopaths, but the mission gods decided that every mission needs at least one good psychopath on staff. The official mission manual, which the Foundation considers classified material, reads:

"A healthy pro-social psychopath is indispensable to the survival of the colony. A normal social ratio (one psychopath to one hundred residents) shall be maintained at all times, whenever possible." It goes on to point out that, in a survival situation, you need someone who can make crisis decisions without panicking, and there's nothing like a good psychopath to fill that job.

During indoctrination, we heard the stories about the first Mars mission, and how they had the two psychopaths along before medical instituted their screening processes. Two psychos to a crew of fifteen. One of them was an anti-social, and there was the rape/murder of the astrogator that put everyone at risk. The trust in the crew fractured, they broke into armed camps. It was the pro-social that spotted the murderer, proved him guilty, spaced him, and saved the mission. As the lecturer told us when he informed us how the teams would be comprised: "It really matters that you've got the right psycho on your team."

I'm still not quite convinced.

Once you've filled your psycho slot, you have to fill up all the others, and all the others have to pass the stability tests with flying colors. Even the smallest blip will get a candidate eliminated. The gods will delay a seed expedition by decades waiting for the right candidate to come along, and have. In our case, we got to the far end and found they'd shipped four people who hadn't been in our indoctrination class; they'd been tracked into the program thirty years ago, then had to wait until the Foundation found enough stable, qualified people to fill the rest of the quota sheet.

"Stability" is a euphemism for "Autism." I wish I was joking. Well, a particular kind of it, anyway. When they said they needed a chronicler, they forgot to mention that the reason they needed one is that, between the psychopath and the thirty-four Autism-spectrum scientists and technicians, I'm the only neurotypical on this crazy planet. I only got to find out about it right before we shipped. They wanted to make sure I was not harboring any prejudices before they broke the news.

Imagine being the only person you know who can *both* feel empathy and communicate it. Imagine being the only person you know who has normal emotional responses. You are locked in a cattle pen with people who have never had a normal relationship in their entire lives, and that pen is surrounded by the most dangerous, gorgeous landscape you have ever seen, and everyone you can talk to finds it "fascinating" or thinks it's "an interesting puzzle." Some of them say "whoa" and look amazed, but they cannot tell that you feel the same way unless you say so, and then repeat it, and then mount a campaign to convince them that you are *not* just trying to make them feel like you care. And the one who *can* look at you and see your feelings, who can make you feel like a human in the company of other humans instead of a babysitter in the company of squalling brats, is neurologically incapable of caring about it.

Thank God my parents were the enlightened kind that got

their daughter a reversible tubal when she hit menarche. At least I will never have to worry about pregnancy. Not that sex is very available around here, not for someone like me. The scientists have their own language around that. Besides, I doubt that I could deal with having to stop in the middle to say "No, really, I do like it. I promise I am not just faking to make you feel better. Yes, that feels wonderful—why do you ask?" And I know I would too. I share a room with one of them—Dr. Bosch, our chief botanist—and I can hear them talking everything out. It sounds to me of football commentators sitting on a porn set.

Proper football, not American football.

But that "disability" is what makes them great at working in these colonies. Stable, unflappable, altogether decent people.

These are the ways the mission gods make sure there will be no power struggles, no matter what. We got that talk the day they put us down for the trip. The strategy has worked perfectly on planetary pioneering missions and long haul space flights for two hundred years. When a system works perfectly for long enough, people stop building in failsafes. There was no plan B for power struggles, because there would not be any power struggles.

Personally, given what transpired over the last couple months, I think the system could use a little work.

By the time we hit the bump, I was already wondering if I might need to go crazy just to stay sane. Make the place feel alive, or at least me, you know? On the other side of our little plasma fence I could see a whole world getting on with the business of being a world. In here, I'm trapped with a collection of stable people doing their stable work. I have never been this bored in my entire life. If this colony were a drink, it would be a glass of warm distilled water with a sprig of parsley in it, for color. A right barrel of laughs, as you say.

Always in my life, I have hated that place in news stories where the journalist, who assumes that no one in her audience earned a passing grade in toilet training, says things like "the turning point came when..." or "that was when everything changed..." or "when he revealed the shocking truth..."

It is insulting. And it is lazy. And I will have no part of it.

It would also be a lie. Because I do not know exactly when the turning point came. I suppose I could guess, and say that it happened when they discovered the planet was poisonous.

"We." It would maybe be better if it was "we." Since they sent me to this god-forsaken end of the universe to provide some human perspective, I will tell to you what happens when thirty-five-plus-one get sent halfway across the galaxy to a planet that has only been surveyed with probes, to sink or swim.

What happens is that we wake up, one by one, and find their place as designated by the mission gods. Acting singly, according to a preordained agenda, they spin up their individual laboratories and projects, and they get on with the work they have come all this way to do. And, during work hours, everything works smoothly, as long as we can stick to our mission.

Our mission is this: We are to conduct a complete analysis of the biosphere so that it may be made safe for human habitation.

Considering where we come from, "safe" is a pretty elastic term. About ninety percent of the surface area of the Earth is unfit for human habitation, and it took us about two hundred thousand years to figure out how to beat our home planet into shape without beating it to death. I imagine that it seemed pretty endless and dangerous to our first grandparents, looking out across endless lands shaped by volcanoes and continental collusions, and then sculpted and softened by grasses and cape buffalo.

It was not something they gave us in the indoctrination packet, but as I have interviewed the worker-bees these past several months in between playing shop assistant, I have built up a scale in my head from "Mars safe" to "Hong Kong safe."

A "Mars safe" environment is one where we cannot survive without bringing our own atmosphere and radiation shields. It's about as bad as a planet can get before it is completely unusable to us.

Above that, you have a Sahara environment, where survival is possible with great ingenuity and lots of biomech assistance—the Berber had camels, we have our robotic labor force to fetch our necessaries.

Moving up the list, you've got the Himalayas, and the Carpathian mountains, and the Aboriginal outback. All very hostile, but completely survivable if you have a clever head and friends with clever heads. It is the definition of our species: humans are the life form that can hack.

Next up the ladder, you find the Amazon and the Congo and the Indian jungles—still hostile, but bursting with food. You just have to make sure not to become food yourself, for predators either macroscopic or microscopic.

After that are the tropical and subtropical islands, with their plentiful fruit and easy game. New Zealand, Hawaii, the Bahamas. A single person with a sharp stick could pretty much make a good life without too much trouble in those places, once upon a time.

But at the pinnacle of habitability, we move into the towns, then into the cities, until you reach Hong Kong level. An environment completely made for and by humans, completely domesticated, filled with living buildings and served by the surrounding lands in a way that puts far less stress on them than trying to beat out a small scale survival. The trick to integrating humans into their environment is to get them to build as high and fast as possible. The more people are in a city, the less toll they take on the surrounding natural land, per capita.

I thought that last part was pretty much crap the first time I heard it, but watching Dr. Wasserman—our planetary ecologist—map out food webs over the last months has made me a believer.

But a poisoned planet? Nobody saw that coming. Nobody could have guessed what it would do to our little boring family.

The trouble we had was that you cannot make a planet filled with neurotoxins fit on the habitability scale. It has breathable air and a magnetic field, so it's no Mars. But it is also bursting with so many proteins to melt your skin, and heavy metals to poison your blood, and prions to rewire your wetware that only a complete idiot would even go out for a walk without a whole body hazmat suit.

When Dr. Prescott briefed us on the situation six months ago, he said we were officially screwed. I'm not sure how official it was. I don't know if he filed a report with the orbital base station for its next probe launch home, scheduled for a year from now. I do know that he made a note in his log about needing to re-evaluate the mission rationale. I like to think that it read "Official: Our entire mission has been sodomized sans lubricant by the capricious whims of evolution. Mission footing re-evaluated."

Because "re-evaluated" is a bang-up euphemism for "redesigned to provoke a civil war."

Well, not exactly a civil war. It wasn't all that civil, and it wasn't much of a war at first. Frankly, watching it unfold was a little bit like watching a box of wet matches trying to light off a fireworks display. Stable, mature people take a long time to get hot under the collar. Which is what the mission gods intended.

It started with the re-evaluation of the mission. Since the notion of making Filbert suitable for human habitation by mapping out the biosphere and finding our niches was clearly ludicrous, our little dysfunctional family gradually explored more radical ideas.

The gods designed the mission to operate in stages:

Stage one: Perform a comprehensive analysis of the biosphere, planet-wide.

Stage two: Deliberation. Everyone (well, everyone not counting me) would argue, at length, about whether to open the planet up for colonization now or later. If now, they would argue about which of the four prefabbed plans we should pursue. If later, when and why, and what it would take to get to "go."

Stage three: Communicate the decision (and all mission records) back to base, then return home if we were so disposed.

Since that was not going to work here, we needed to improvise. And since all the previous colonies had been established in the Sol system—the Proxima disaster notwithstanding—we were in unexplored territory philosophically as well as practically.

I trust you will excuse the discursive style. I am attempting to collate and compile notes and recordings from a very eventful time, and I find I have to jump around to make it all coherent.

So, there was the announcement. And, after some initial

not-quite-shouting, Dr. Prescott ceded the floor to Dr. Galbraith, the official mission commander, and our resident psychopath, and the only person here I can't stand. It's a personal matter, not important to anything, so I won't dwell on it here. According to mission law, which we all swore to abide by, the mission commander is the king of our little country. A despot. An absolute monarch. At least, provided he confines his despotism to the territory defined in the (thankfully narrow) mission protocols.

He stood in the center of the circle and waited until the rest of us gave up and stopped trying to talk over each other.

"Look," he said, "we can dance and sling all the crap we want, but we're not going to solve anything. We need answers and some serious ideas. How deep does this go..."

"All the way down. It's in the goddamn *soil*, Darren."

"Maybe. Maybe. Or maybe you've just let your fingers do the walking so your rectum does the talking. The soil back home is a stew of pathogens and lead and cadmium and we managed to evolve perfectly well there. So try pulling your fingers out of your ass and give 'em a good lick and hold 'em up to the wind, and get me some bloody data and some creativity. That goes for the rest of you too. That's what they picked all you people for, right? Brilliantness and methodicalness and creativeness and all that other messiness, right? I hope so, cause they sure didn't pick you for your personalities. Stop jumping to conclusions and get me some goddamn options."

He looked straight at me. Sitting in my little seat in the back, I got chills. He always knew exactly when to abuse them and exactly when to coddle them. Now I was the target, and I half dreaded what might next come out of his mouth.

"Xiyi, this includes you. Come up with anything you can.

Bring it. We'll meet back here in two weeks, and we'll sit in this room until we come up with something. I don't know about all of you, but I didn't come here for the scenery and I sure as hell don't want to retire here. We got a job to do, so get to it and don't let me catch you talking hopeless."

Nobody grumbled after he left. We simply each looked at the other for a moment or two, then began breaking up into our different teams. Nobody asked for my help, and nothing urgent seemed to be happening, so I went to walk the perimeter to make sense out of what Dr. Prescott had just told us.

I remember looking through the fence and thinking it was all a bad dream. The whole expedition. I could feel the wind off the mountain cool against my neck, and it chilled me clean through, even though it was summer. Above me, the midday sun painted the patchy overcast with the spectrum of depression.

I did *not* sign up for this. I did not exactly sign up for any of it, to be truthful, but I did have a choice. I could have found another job somewhere. In some part of the world, there would have been someone who would see a novelist as an asset instead of a security risk. I remembered sitting across from that human slug Wanda Laird, and how she made me feel like a bug she wanted to squish, and tried to make me think she would ruin me if I refused.

But I also remembered thinking about what my name would look like in the history books. How it would be my account you all would read. My voice that would give narrative cohesion to the dry collection of logs. My observations that would give substance to the characters.

No sane, intelligent person would refuse. I came because I wanted to.

As storm clouds gathered in the valley below me, I wished I had found the courage to admit that to myself before I came. It might have made a difference, somehow.

It was supposed to be a heroic tale, like the *Ramayana*. I was Valmiki, bringing the great tale to all who came after. If I knew it was going to turn out this way, if I even thought it was possible, I might not have come.

Now, we would go down as a footnote. A failed expedition. "The official record shows that the Filbert expedition never stood a chance. Fortunately, all of the other ten expeditions succeeded." The world outside the shield was trying to kill us all. And maybe there was no way to stop it. No way to win. But it looked so bloody beautiful, I wondered if I would really mind. When my soul melted back into the universe, would I think it was a waste? Would I miss my name?

That was six months ago. Things, since then, have changed.

Expedition: Filbert
Mission Day 237
Mission Historian Personal Perspective
Year 2253 of the Common Era

A WEEK ON FROM THEN, Mission Day fifty dating from when I was released from quarantine, I was collecting the food for my lunch from the mess line, when I spied something wrong.

Or, well, at least unusual.

Drs. Stella Bosch and Jonathan Davidson were not what I would call friends. The nature of their work demanded the semi-frequent intercourse of their routines—she being the chief of our botanical sciences division and he being the head of molecular bioengineering and fabrication—but they had never developed the familial affection that the rest of us had acquired during our boot camp time and our stay here on-planet. They normally treated one another with icy professional courtesy. When I found them huddled together at lunchtime mess a week later, I considered it my duty to intrude.

"I hope not to be intruding," I said, setting my plate down next to Stella. Asserting roommate privilege flummoxed her a little, and it took her a moment to figure out what to say, by which time I was already on my way. "Something is going on here. As mission chronicler I demand confidential access, as authorized by general order sixty-two." They shifted uncomfortably. I smirked. "I may be persuaded to pay with chocolate."

"Oh, well, if you're gonna pay in chocolate, I..." Stella stopped, reconsidered her words, and gave me a dirty look. "Wait, where the hell did you get chocolate way out here?"

"I brought the formula in my personal data allowance. I can print out about ten grams during my weekly time allotment."

Stella pointed her fork at me. "We're going to have to talk about the roommate's code, you and me, girly."

"After." I looked at Jonathan. "You too. I am entitled to know what you two are doing. Deviations from normal routine. You both hate each other. What draws you into cahoots?"

They exchanged nervous glances, then made a set of hand signals at one another. It was not a sign language, not exactly. It was a gesture-based vocabulary that the ASDs had all learned to communicate emotions without words, in the same way that neurotypicals read facial expressions. I knew enough of it to recognize that their fingers were roughly approximating the emotions on their faces. Trepidation, frustration, dread. I found myself wishing I had failed to ask.

"Stop dithering. Tell me." Not for the first time, I wished I had the facility with spoken English as I do with written. I find it embarrassing now as I write, listening to the recordings, hearing the stilted mangle I make of words that fill my head with such clarity. I have never quite been able to shake the tonal grammar of my native language, and my tongue does not cooperate with the speed it should, and my wit always lags three seconds behind my mouth. "Jonathan. What vexes you?"

"We found the problem this morning." He rubbed his face, shaking his head against his hand, as if he had just discovered that all was lost in the world. "Well, at least, I think it's the problem. And we should have spotted it before we ever came here. I designed the probe, I should have…dammit. One of those things that is so simple, so uniform, it never occurred to me to build in a control. I didn't even find it by checking for it, I just stumbled onto it this morning…"

"So, what is it?"

He held up his left hand, pointed to it with his right. "This."

"Your hand?"

"The left hand. We're on a left-handed planet."

"I am left-handed," I said, "I think more than half the people here are left-handed. Why is this a problem?"

"Not you and me. The planet. The molecules. Everything. It's called 'chirality'. You've heard of it?"

I shook my head.

"It's a bias in how molecules form in a given environment, and nobody knows exactly why it happens. Maybe something to do with the stellar nebula, or the planet's magnetic field, or maybe to do with the crystalline structure in deep sea vents where life forms, or the order of reactions in the way a planet self-organizes. Nobody knows for sure. We know there are about a thousand ways to induce structural polarity reversals in chiral molecules and..."

He stopped. I had made the ASD finger sign that meant "huh?" The most useful ASD sign I had learned up to that point, that was.

He cleared his throat. "Okay, short layman's version: in the Sol system, and everywhere else, the molecules that make life up—the proteins, especially—are overwhelmingly right-handed. They all fit together in a certain way, because of their shapes, and this fit is what makes life work. It governs the way they react, the metabolism, everything. Sugars are usually left-handed, but since they're easy to break down, that's not as big a problem. For some reason that we don't know yet, this planet is almost all left-handed proteins and right-handed sugars. That means that the proteins fold differently, and everything works like it was in a mirror. When those molecules line up with our molecules, some things have no effect at all, because nothing fits. Sometimes, they have a neutral effect, where enough works that the reaction can take place. I'll bet some of the sugars will wind up working this way. And some things, maybe most things, will be poisonous, because they'll react half-way and leave us with weird metabolic waste products, or they'll make a normal energy exchange a leech exchange..."

I made the sign again. Stella took pity on me.

"Xiyi, do you know how carbon monoxide poisoning works?"

"I think so. The monoxide bonds with hemoglobin and crowds out oxygen, and you suffocate from the inside out."

"Right. What Jonathan's saying is that a wrong-handed protein or amino acid could screw up cellular metabolism in that same kind of way."

"And that makes them poisonous."

"That's the theory." Jonathan took a drink of his synthetic coffee, then grimaced at it as if it had betrayed him.

"So, what can we do about it?"

"That's what I'm working on."

He brought me up to speed. By the time he had, I felt sick to my stomach.

Transcendence

In their final moment, the city lights etched themselves into a photograph that no human eye would ever see. A photograph containing every street, every thread, every connection in the city. A map, infinitely detailed, perfectly captured and encoded in ultra-dense quinary notation, losslessly compressed, and stored away in the most secure databank in the world.

And why not? A map of such precision, of a landscape of such intricacy as to capture the attention of cartography enthusiasts and chaotic mathematicians and hold them for years on end? Such a map deserved a prized position in any databank.

And so it had.

It was not the first map of its kind. It would not be the last. But it was, and would forever remain, utterly unique.

Even though, in the entire vastness of the universe, no human would ever study it.

Chapter 4

Soul Concerns

THEY HADN'T BEEN WARNED about the boring people yet. Those were in a separate class, and integration would come toward the end of the training. At the beginning, subjects had been grouped by basic personality orientation, with the gregarious in one track, the reserved in another, and the stable ones in a third. Teams would be picked and mixed at the end of the second six week cycle, based on who scored how on the tests, who survived the different evaluations, and who had the gumption to stick through the intellectual and emotional whiplash.

After Solly's departure, and the falling away of most of the rest of her core cluster in the weeks following, Xiyi found herself more and more sticking with Dar for company. Aside from Daimler, her writing coach, he was the only person with whom she had any kind of real connection through the bulk of her training.

She and Dar had a similar way of looking at the world. Detached, almost. An outsider's view. She thought it odd, from time to time, since he wasn't an outsider—he was as much an insider as you could get with the Foundation—but he had a casual aloofness that seemed to always suggest he was in on some grand joke that everyone would get to laugh at someday.

And he was never short on sharp observations, or witticisms. She happily pilfered them, plugging them into the journals she was keeping religiously as part of her training for the mission. Twice a day, just like a ship's captain, reporting on the minutiae of her minutes, with particular attention to the interpersonal dynamics around her, and sprinkled liberally with her own opinion and experience. It was different from her novels. More intimate, more deliberate, and with an audience looking over her shoulder. Her instructor reviewed her entries twice a week, and made technique suggestions, which she dutifully applied to the next round.

At the end of the first six week cycle, they had their first week-long mix cycle. The different personality groups were all thrown together for their first seminar in mission law. Unbeknownst to the candidates, their every interaction was closely studied to identify personality combinations that might prove detrimental to the social health of the mission.

The integration week exhausted Xiyi like nothing she'd run into before. Dealing with the reserved and stable populations made her head hurt. The sheer amount of effort that went into making herself understood, and making sure she understood properly what they were trying to communicate—at great length, with many qualifiers, and with ridiculous amounts of nervous trepidation—left her feeling like a badly squeezed, half-rotten orange.

"Pay attention to your own reactions over the next week," Daimler told her. "They will give you the information you need to develop your coping techniques. Each team will be made up mostly of these two groups, so you'll be dealing with them a lot. You'll have at least one more gregarious person along with you, possibly as many as six, depending. But you're going to need to deal with the other sorts, or you're going to wash out." He didn't have to add *and we know what that means*. She was already adding it on to everything everyone said to her. Everywhere she turned, there seemed to be someone cautioning her about this or warning her about that, and she wished they'd all just get the hell out of the way so she could figure things out for herself.

But Dar was a rock she could lean on. She'd never needed one before. Wasn't sure she even needed one now. She'd always managed to muddle through quite well on her own, thank you very much. But even so, having him around with a quick quip and a sly smile kept her energized, made her feel good about being herself and doing this crazy-risky thing, and helped her forget she'd been strong-armed into it. They took to spending late evenings in the med center, trading massages and debriefing from the day's sessions, doing homework together—though his was very different from hers, as he wasn't being trained for chronicling duty.

He had kind hands, and a gentle manner, and seemed to anticipate her in an almost preternatural way. They fit together, like puzzle pieces. She'd never had many close friends—a side effect of being a writer, she supposed, her head stuck always in observation mode. But Dar understood that, and she felt as if, on those evenings, they weren't in the med center at all, but instead situated high up on a balcony overlooking a city, trading stories about the happenings on the street below from their place of privileged vision.

It felt good to have a co-conspirator. It made the mindfuck of indoctrination seem bearable. Especially when he dug into her exhausted muscles with the hot oil and those subtle hands that seemed strong enough to strip the sinews from her bones without ever breaking the skin.

"Bad week?" He could read it by braille in her traps, she was sure.

"Awful. I have not the proper words."

"Introverts getting you down?"

"No. Tiring, though, yes. Very tiring."

"Us actual people-folks are gonna have to stick together. When they announce teams, be sure to get in tight with your human-types so you don't get sucked dry by the vampires." Dar's favorite word for anyone who kept to themselves. Xiyi found herself hard-pressed to disagree.

She winced as he found the hard knot that rode directly under her bra strap. "I wish they would put us both on the same team." He found the shape of it and gauged the correct pressure to use. "Oooh, right there. Ah. Ow. Mmm... would make life so much easier, at the other end."

"Won't happen, sweetcakes. To much power concentration. They're watching us all the time, you know. Probably listening to us right now. They'll never put two friends from the same sociability class on the same team. That's a power block..."

"But the stables have couples and..."

"The stables aren't what the gods'd call 'sentimental.' But what are you?"

"Neurotypical? Gregarious? Alliance broker?"

"So trust me. Remember that trouble they had on the first Lunar colony, when things fell apart because of some kind of adultery thing?"

"How old, again, did you say you were?" There was no way she could tell by looking. Like everyone else who'd lived past forty, he looked on the young side of middle-aged. Perpetually at the peak of his game.

He chuckled. "I stopped counting at a hundred twenty. Didn't seem much point. Drinking age is the last important birthday anyway, right?"

Some part of her unlocked at his words, and she felt herself begin the long slide into a stupor. Her stress began to melt beneath his hands, as if he'd just knocked down the wall that had been holding her back. She realized it was because she'd always felt a little bit inadequate next to him, her only a pup not yet to thirty, and him, her best friend, well north of the century mark. What he found interesting about her was anyone's guess, but his reassurance that it didn't matter to him made it easier to accept the relaxation he was pushing into her thoracics. "I guess so."

"Damn right. So that was when they started filtering neurotypicals out of all seed-group expeditions. They're taking a big risk mixing it up now, they won't make it worse by pre-loading power blocks or conflicts of interest. Is this okay?"

"Three centimeters left? There. Oh oh ow, softer please? I hear they intend to pick ten teams."

"Hmph."

"You have heard something else?"

"Ten expeditions is what I heard. I expect they'll pick one team."

"Huh? Say again, please?"

"What they need is going to be the same for each expedition, right? Geology, molecular bioengineering, microbiology, operations, histology, cladistics, ecology, botanical sciences, and command. If you have a crack team, why not send the same team to each location?"

A shudder crept up her neck, as if she'd just stepped on a

slug. As the weeks passed, she had come to think of indoctrination as a kind of boot camp disguised as boarding school as the mission gods honed and molded her and her classmates into perfect excursionists. Through the whole experience, they had kept her jumping from one foot to the other fast enough that she barely had a chance to think through the disquiet Solly had sown in her. Now, it slid down upon her like an ice-riven mountainside.

"Ugh. That's grotesque. I just...ew. Ugh."

"What? Why?"

"Well, to start off, it is against every civilized law ever placed in the books..."

"And that law will apply halfway across the galaxy?"

"It is against *mission* law. No cloning. They send a supply of robot seeds if we need extra hands..."

"Again, so what? It's against the mission law for us to do it on site there, because they can't possibly design the teams to be harmonious if we're all throwing them out of balance, or if we feel like we can be replaced. How can you have trust in a situation like that—when, say your mission commander doesn't like your position in an argument—when he could just shoot you and make another one. That kind of thing would never work, and you know it. Nobody would work to capacity under that kind of threat. That's a self-enforcing law. Doesn't mean that every probe won't have the same crew."

He spoke as if it were all just a banal philosophical exercise, instead of a hard fact of life they'd all be running up against in a couple more months. She felt her whole body tensing up as if she just heard someone following her on a park path at night. "They said they weren't doing that..."

"They could be lying."

"You do not believe that. If you did, you wouldn't still be

in the program."

"Why not? If they did I'd get to go to every one of those new planets..."

"You would not. This is nonsense. You would have just nine twins, and then they would go, except...there would not be alive with in them anymore..."

"Why not?"

"You'd each have only a tenth of a soul."

"Wait. My soul?" He chuckled.

"Yes." She slid out from under his hands and sat up, wrapping the table sheet around her body. "Your soul. You have a soul, and if you dilute it like that..."

"Why would that hurt me? Don't identical twins happen? Are they sharing the same soul? Or are there two souls because they split before they're born?"

"Of course not. They have their own souls..."

"Wait wait, hold on, walk through this with me. How? When is it that you get a soul?"

"No, not like that. More it is like..." She was a writer. All she needed was a good metaphor to make it all make sense. She was obviously dealing with a materialist, which bothered her a bit, since she'd never had any reason to think that Dar wasn't just an ordinary person with reasonable ideas. "Your brain is like an antenna. A radio, and tuned to the particular frequency, and that frequency is the frequency for your particular own soul."

"And that soul is...?"

"Call it a signal. A piece of the universe incarnating in through you. When you develop, as like a fetus and up till a toddler, you still are tuning in, and so which is why your personality is not quite in focus. Fuzzy, I suppose. Blurry. And if you get brain damage or one of those old diseases that make your brain decay..."

"Degenerative geriatric conditions?" He sat down in a chair a few meters off, appearing perfectly relaxed. "Like Alzheimer's?"

"Yes. Yes, like that. So your tuning goes...I don't know...out, and what makes you you is gets lost. The signal decays...or, maybe...you cannot manifest the signal. Your focus, that decays."

"I'm with you so far." He nodded encouragement. No note of condescension or tolerance in it, which helped. She suddenly realized that his first doctorate was in neurology, so she was probably jumping all over his sacred cows, but he wanted her to continue, and she couldn't have shut up anyway. Her whole inner being was screaming.

"But if there is more than one of you? With an identical brain? Identical memories and everything? Then there too many receivers are for the signal. Your life would become gray. You would stop being you..."

"Okay. For the sake of argument, why would that happen? Wouldn't the source of the signal—God?"

"The universe."

"Wouldn't the universe be so overwhelming, so powerful that no one receiver could ever drain it? Not even multiples of the same frequency? Wouldn't it be like a radio station, where the broadcast goes everywhere, and any given receiver only picks up a tiny piece of it?"

She shook her head. "It is...more direct than that. Like a point-to-point. Here..." She tied the sheet across her sternum and fished her handheld out of her bag under the table, and started searching for her class notes from the first session of her 101-level bioengineering class. "Here it is. The number of potential humans, taking all factors into account, is approximately one sexvigintillion. About the same number as the atoms in the entire universe. Identical twins share the same DNA, yes, this is true. But they do not have the same methylation quotient. Epigenome, you know, yes?"

"Yes, I know methylation."

"Nor the same development. It all is different, and that is what tunes them for different souls. Makes them different people. Why would the universe do that, if two receivers for the same signal were as good as one? What if every receiver is different for a reason?"

"Interesting theory." He folded his fingers together and appeared to consider it. "So each copy would be like a kind of zombie?"

"I suppose. Half-alive."

"But this isn't a problem with our star travel method because you die here and wake up somewhere else, a perfect copy, tuned to the same frequency, so you still have your soul?"

"Yes." She shuddered again at the thought of dying, but that was just normal meat-qualms. A survival instinct. It had nothing to do with the matter at hand. She shoved it aside for later.

"Solly didn't think so."

"Well, no, but Solly was...is Prophetic-Messiaist. The desert religions, they all think the soul is created just for the body, and if you die, it goes on. For them a resurrection trip would be a body with no soul. Or maybe the same body with a new soul. A clone. Something alive, and burdened with the sins and memories of a past life they never lived."

Dar nodded. "But either way it's not them, so they wash out, because they are not willing to risk dying by suicide, and insulting God."

"Yes, yes, that is it exactly. But I am not saying anything

so...primitive. Well, perhaps this is not fair."

"I suppose it depends whether you believe the universe is an eternal self, or an eternal unfolding. You believe the former?"

"Yes. So perhaps it just is different." Xiyi stopped. She felt like she'd been swimming somewhere, but had foundered under a wave, and gotten turned around. What had she wanted to solve? That sense of disquiet about her own soul in this enterprise, yes, that was it. "They simply cannot send us all out to different planets. In the contracts...hold on..." She pulled up her admissions contract, and read over the fine print. "Here. Section twelve, paragraph twenty-eight. 'In deference to the International Convention on the Continuity of Personhood, the Foundation guarantees that all uploads shall be held in escrow by the ICCP, and all transfers shall be supervised thereby. No unauthorized copies of the neural map shall be made or attempted, and all backup copies (from both current and previous iterations) shall be expunged from all ICCP databases upon transfer to the spacecraft...' and it goes on to describe how they're will be preventing the craft from transmitting pirate copies back. So I was right. They will not do such a thing."

"Well, you know how to be sure?"

"How?"

"When they pick your team, refuse to progress until they show you the mission spec. Environmental, planet name, that kind of thing. If the planet you wake up on matches the one they told you about, you know you're fine. I can't imagine they found two planets similar enough that they could dodge around that, and they can't erase that particular memory unless they have you actively accessing it when you're in the machine."

"You are absolutely sure about this?"

"Completely."

Xiyi made a note to herself. As she did, she felt the tension melt back down to background level. Now she knew how to figure out what she was up against. Pressure and blackmail or not, she still wanted to go, would give anything to go. She'd even give her soul, if she thought it was something she could live without. But since she didn't, since giving it up would mean losing the part of herself that most wanted to go...

This was better. This, she could work with. Now, if she made the cut, maybe she really could go. Maybe, at the end of the junket, she could even come back.

Dar clasped her shoulder. "There. Feeling better?"

"I think so. Yes. Better."

"Good. My turn?"

"I guess so."

Dar stripped down and draped a fresh sheet on the table. As her fingers dug into his deltoids she realized that he wasn't tense at all, and a shadow of that uneasy feeling came back to her, as if she were in the presence of something not quite human.

Movement

There was no "now."
There was no "then."
There was no "was."
There was no "am."
There was only "will be."

The map, in all its inimitable, immutable grandeur, slid into its slot in the archive. On either side, and above and below, other maps nestled. And outside of them, still others. Maps of different cities, of different paradigms, and of different sorts of structures entirely. A microcosm of cartography, ranging across every substrate. A complete guide for building a new world.

The archive docked with a ringship in polar orbit. The ringship pushed its way to stellar north, clear of the more intense debris fields, and aimed for its destination.

And then, like a child on a summer day, it blew an enormous bubble, and stepped inside.

And vanished.

Chapter 5

Parlay

Expedition: Filbert
Mission Day 238
Mission Historian Personal Perspective
Year 2253 of the Common Era

THE AUDIO RECORDS OF JONATHAN'S explanation can be found attached to this digest, should any of you reading care to access the primary source material I am using to bolster my memories of the event. It turns out I did not need them for anything but wording check. Some things burn into the soul.

Doctor Davidson took hours explaining to me the fix we were in. By the time he was done, I was sure we would have to abandon Filbert. The next week, I walked in circles as much as my mind ran in circles, running up against the fence in every free moment, looking out at the alien world that I now wanted to call home. I had fallen in love, here. The purple vegetation, the glowing rivers, the gas giant—we call it Fred—in the sky casting us into eclipse one day out of twelve, everything just strange enough, just new enough, that it did not feel like Earth.

It did not feel angry.

Just peaceful. Just beautiful. Deadly, most certain, but

deadly as the sea is. As the sky. The kind of deadly that does not wish you harm, but just happens to be, by being itself. That kind of deadly, that kind of danger, made sense to me in a way that malice did not, even though I have known more of malice than anything else. I suppose that is the way of things when you have only three decades behind you.

I spent those next long days on the perimeter circuit, alone. Not good for my mental health. I do not like being alone. I do not do well with it. There had not been much in the way of R&R, but all of my social time had gone the way of pollen in a spring rain. With all nine departments operating every hour of the night and day (thirty-six hours here), I counted any time alone as a blessing, except for the deep gnawing emptiness at the center of me.

Not for the first time, I wondered if they might really have duplicated me. If another me had a hold of a piece of my soul somewhere. During indoctrination, a once-friend told me I could verify that they did not duplicate me by checking the mission details against where I ended up, and I thought it had worked, but how could I know for sure? Perhaps I was the clone that went where she expected, and another one of me woke up somewhere else, and was told they'd reassigned her.

It would make sense. It would explain the gray haze that had settled down in my center. A stone in my belly. The dread.

I felt as if I could be the last lonely stalk of barely after a harvest, and yet could not feel the winter winds. Such loathing filled me for all my fellows there. The thought that what we had come to do could not be done, with only some creative miracle standing between ourselves and the abyss.

Is this the price for coming to love people you did not think you could stand? Of investing in their dreams as if they were your own? I knew I did not want to see their faces, faces they would not easily read, but that I would, as soon as they received the news from each other. As the floater, I was obliged to secrecy.

And, I reasoned, none of them needed me to add to their burdens. They would all find out, soon enough. My heart felt as if it were a rose petal, doused in liquid nitrogen, and like to shatter at the smallest breeze.

I heard footsteps approaching. I turned to see Dr. Galbraith striding to join me, his average frame topped by a fire of tight-curled blond lit by the noon. My stomach soured further, and I wished I had never come on this junket. Hopeless situations and me, we are not good friends and never have been. Still less pathological liars, and Dr. Galbraith was definitely one of those.

Of all the people I least wished to speak to, he was the paragon.

"Xiyi, good."

"As you say." I turned back to the view, wishing that the world on the other side wasn't poisonous. It would be a fine place running thick with children, dotted with parks and farms, and still wild enough to be worth the word. The human spirit loves the richness of the city, but some part of it craves the challenge of the wilderness. Mine was sick with reflected failure.

But no matter how I tried, I could not shut out Dr. Galbraith.

"Wasserman's going to give his report in an hour."

"Such as it may be."

"I trust you'll be there?"

"Of course."

"Do you know what he plans to say?"

I did not answer. I knew he had run this conversation

through at least five times in his mind, and knew every permutation. I did not want to give him the satisfaction.

"Xiyi, I can throw you in the brig and yank your printer time for not cooperating."

"And you can remind me that I have no soul, and that I am stupid, a little girl swimming in deep waters, and that I was lucky ever to be selected. Yes, you can do many things. Perhaps you can jump into the fence, save us both the trouble of avoiding each other. I would consider it a favor."

"That's hardly fair..."

"Perhaps you also know what is fair. You *are* the mission commander." I turned from him and walked along the fence, following the track I had assiduously worn into the red soil.

He raised his voice. "Do I need to remind you what happened to Solly?"

Of every come back, every lever I might have expected, it was the one I had not steeled myself against. I stopped dead in my tracks. "Solly quit."

"Yes he did. Because he couldn't take it. He wasn't good enough for this job, and he knew it."

"And so?"

"So maybe," he crossed his arms and his eyes squinted, just a little, "you should have quit too."

I was missing something. Something in his tone. "I did not quit." I turned and tried to walk away.

He followed, kept pace right on beside me. "He couldn't make it out here. I knew it. You knew it. It was only a matter of time before he realized it. Face it, sweet cheeks, Solly didn't have the stones for a job like this, and I made sure he realized it."

"You..." Of course it was him. I hated myself for not seeing before. That day when Solly packed up, how he did not even look at either of us. I found myself stopping again. If I let him see my anger, he would win. That was what his kind did, how they worked. Using your self's humanity against it.

"Perhaps I should have helped you realize it too."

"Son of a bastard."

"I can work with that." His voice was right behind me. His hand closed around my elbow. "It was better for him that way, and he probably got a sweet gig with Mannix Spaceways or something. He was a good kid. Now listen, and for God's sake pay attention. When I walk in there I'm walking into the shitter. This is the kind of thing that can wreck a colony, and unless you want to see these people at each other's throats, unless you want to see us all shot home with nothing to show for it, unless you want this to go into the toilet because of you, then you need to tell me what you know."

"Dar, I...No. It was a confidence. You will find out..."

"What matters in there is how we spin it. I mean, what do you think happens if we get the worst possible news: It's impossible, unethical, and dangerous to even think about proceeding. These people, some of them waited *half a century* for this chance. And if we have the worst news, we could have a war on our hands. Do you understand what that means?"

His words shook me right down to the center. My ability to speak almost left me. "So you say, as what if, the news is bad. You will know soon."

"If I know now, I can plan. If you make me wait, I have to improvise, and we both know that doesn't always work."

My arms wrapped around myself. I did not will it. I did not want it. They simply did it, as if my body would fall to pieces if they failed. His grip softened, holding me instead of restraining me. The breeze whipped cool streaks on my face, and I found I had to grit my teeth to stop myself from melting into him, or bolting from him.

He was not my friend. Not anymore. But I thought he might be the only hope we had. So, God help me, I told him everything. And then he thanked me, and walked away, as if he were just going for some coffee.

AN HOUR LATER, AT THE meeting we had dubbed "The First Filbert Planetary Summit" (for a joke), the news was not just from molecular bioengineering, or histology, or bacteriology. No. There was much more, and much worse. Only the department heads—and me—were present, for reasons Dr. Galbraith designated "rumor control." I thought at the time that he just did not want more people than he could easily control in the mess for such an important meeting.

Geology went last. Dr. Thorndale Wasserman briefed us on the circadian and geological issues as a coda to his report on general planetary ecology—we already knew they presented a serious difficulty, but I do not think any of us appreciated the full scale of the challenge until he laid it out for us.

A stout man, who always smelled as if he had walked off a creosote plantation, he was close to the normal end of the spectrum. A sharp chess player, but not quite so good at poker, which made him a reliable source of extra printer time in the manufacturing hut.

Among litany of unpleasant news, he told us that Filbert had a volatile magnetic field, something else that the probes couldn't catch due to limitations that nobody had known would be limitations. This meant we had two more problems: the local environment experienced unpredictable radiation spikes much more frequently than on Earth, and the local biosphere was adapted to it in a number of nasty ways.

On Earth, we have sophisticated DNA error correction

machinery built into our cells to deal with mutations. On Filbert, much of the native life uses heavy metals to shield their nuclei from the radiation. Preventions, on top of corrections. Another reason for the poisoned biosphere. Different environments breed different life forms. In our case, though, the radiation would present a new problem for colonists. They would have to live under a dome.

Filbert was looking less and less hospitable with every passing sentence.

"In sum, as far as I can tell, we have four options if we want to colonize this planet: First, we raze the biosphere and terraform Filbert from scratch. Obviously this option introduces some profound ethical difficulties which I'm sure you've all thought of already.

"Second, we terraform *in situ*. This is a higher risk strategy, and it's never been attempted before, but it is quite possible that we could encourage the native biosphere to exist in parallel with the one we introduce. Plants, insects, bacteria, animals. Competition between them would happen only at the mineralogical level—above that, the food for one set of organisms would be inedible to the other set. If we could prove the concept, it would provide a paradigm for future seed colonies should they run into similar problems. The risks and ethical problems are obvious.

"Third, we create a limited-presence foothold. We lay groundwork for enough infrastructure to handle perhaps fifty thousand people in a domed city, sterilize the requisite amount of farmland and re-seed it with our own bacteria, putting everything together as a quarantine zone. Then, we leave the residents to sort the problem out in a generation or two, once their numbers have grown enough that it's worth the trouble.

"Fourth, we set up a proper survey to catalog the planet,

and we leave it here to run. We go home, collect our honorarium, and decide what to do next."

Thorndale turned off his projector, shrugged, made the ASD finger signal for resigned uncertainty (basically: "I have no idea what to do") and sat down.

Christiana—Doc Sansa—threw up her hands. "Well, that's us screwed then, eh? We should bring in all the grunts, let 'em get a good whiff of the compost. Bugger."

Galbraith stood, clapping his hands as if he were trying to attract the notice of a class of unruly children. "Stow that shit, Chris. Come on, people, I said I want options. Are these the only four? What else did you come up with? We've got enough PhDs in this outpost to wallpaper a hotel. Show me what you got. Impress me."

Nobody said anything. Everyone looked at everyone else.

Galbraith's eyes fell on me, and I found myself speaking without even wanting to breathe. "On Earth, humans have the occupying of only ten percent of the surface, yes? Is it perhaps possible that we could develop one of the continents for ourselves, and leave for the others for the native species?"

"Okay, that's five. Keep 'em coming. Once we've got them on the board, we'll dicker."

Dr. Hakiyama, head of virology, raised her left eyebrow and said, in as patronizing a manner as she could manage: "Why Darren, my love, your board is so bright and full. However shall we compete with it?" Which drew attention to the fact that Galbraith had neither turned on the board, nor did he hold so much as a pin and clay tablet for taking notes.

"Forget it," I said. "I will see to it." I left my seat and turned on the display, setting myself up as the note-taker. I am, after all, the chronicler.

In short order, our few options appeared on the board.

"There is one other option we should consider..." Davidson, the molecular bioengineering head, shifted in his seat as if he'd just had a wet fart, and itched. He would not meet anyone's eyes.

"Let it out," Galbraith said, "This is an open forum."

Davidson drew his breath in, and held it. He looked around, as if he would find help in the faces he couldn't read. His own held shame the likes of which I have never seen, as if he were about to suggest sacrificing babies to appease the gods of Filbert.

When he opened his lips again, I wished he had. He said: "What if we re-engineered ourselves and the colonists to fit in here?"

As if he'd struck a match in a methane tank, the room went incandescent. I could not follow the shouted outrage, the accusations and counter-accusations. I did not manage to write it all down, but it turned out not to matter.

Galbraith lifted a chair and smashed it down in the center of the circle. The solid polymer didn't smash, but the *thunk* rang through the dome. "Everybody SHUT UP! You!" He shot his hand out at Hal Prescott, looming over Davidson and looking like he was about to box the engineer's ears. "Sit down. The rest of you shut up."

Darren Galbraith in fury is a sight to behold. Terrible as Lei Gong summoning a hurricane. Everyone complied. I found myself typing again. *#6: Re-engineering human presence to fit environment.*

"Now, we're going to go through these points one at a time, and then we're going to go through everything else we can think of. You were all selected for your stability and intelligence, right? Well start showing some."

"Goddammit, Darren," Stella Bosch said through her

hands. "why don't you shut the hell up. I know you don't have feelings but the rest of us do, okay? We're screwed. We're completely screwed and we've wasted the better part of the century on this...this...fiasco! Why don't you give us a few days to come to grips with the fact that we died for nothing, huh?"

"Because we only died for nothing if we quit. You and me and all the rest of us, right now, are going to figure out what we can do." He looked around the circle of shame-faced scientists. He took a deep breath, walked out of the circle, and started wandering around the hall. "A hundred years ago, we couldn't even dream about being here. Two hundred fifty years ago, they almost gave up space travel as stupid. We have lived our lives doing the impossible, every one of us. Black magic resurrectionists. Zombies. Life engineers. Worldbuilders. Gods by other names. We came here in a little dinky can no bigger than the circle you're sitting in now. Now, maybe we're beat. Maybe we've met our match. Maybe we've failed.

"But you all know as well as I that science is the codification of failure. It's an edifice *built* on failure. Our entire species exists because our ancestors managed to fail just enough to learn better." He reached the far wall, turned right. He took long, thoughtful strides along the perimeter of the room. Circling us all like a hungry tiger.

"What would have happened if the Greeks hadn't run twenty-six miles from one battle to another, in full gear, to head off the Persian attack? What if the Apollo team listened to 'it can't be done' when that ship blew up on the launchpad? What kind of world would we have if President Orin hadn't quit her comfy job and put her life on the front line in front of those Marines in Luna City? What kind of life would we have if Mannix hadn't beat the people hunting her and invented the drive ship? We are out here *because* it's impossible. We are giants standing on the shoulders of people with more heart and more grit than whole nations had before them. And every single one of you has more brains than any ten Einsteins. We are the best that our species has ever seen, and it's a species full of people whose names are written across the entire galaxy. So don't you tell me it can't be done."

He reached my position, winked at me. It shocked me out of my trance. He turned right and entered the circle.

"I am in command here. By law. Which you all swore to abide by. And as far as I'm concerned all options are on the table. Now. We are going to sit here, and we are going to formulate a plan, or two plans, or a dozen plans, and we're going to hash through the ethics, and the feasibility, and when we leave here we're going to be ready to do what humans do. And then we're going to leave here, and brief our staffs, and *do our jobs*. We're going to look straight back up at the universe and say 'Ha! You think you can get us that way? Well, fuck you. We're smarter than you. Checkmate, asshole.' Because that's what humans do." He sat down, crossed his arms, looked around the circle. His eyes dazzled like the sky on a bright clear night, and I recognized the Dar I used to think I knew, back before. He was flying. Drunk and joyful. Ready to beat the world into submission with a smile and a dance. "Now, the floor is open. Let's hear it all—one at a time, and be articulate. If any of you starts with the indignation or the blubbering, I'll have Xiyi over there mention in the record that you're a complete nancy that slipped through by mistake."

Hal Prescott shrugged. "Fine, I'll start. Frankly, I don't think there's a good option in the bunch. We're blundering around in the dark here and we're clearly under-equipped. Our best option is to redesign the survey protocols and report back to base. If we can avoid this situation in the future, I call it a win. We've proved the travel method works over long distances. The ship's been in orbit for almost a year now, she'll take another two years to harvest enough antimatter from the Van Allen belts to have enough fuel to get us home, so we use that time to do the redesign, then we load up our message in a bottle, go to sleep, and shoot ourselves back home."

I put his proposal on the board as option seven. I had to type fast, lest the conversation run away faster than I could follow.

"Poppycock," Christiana huffed. "Until we catalog this planet top-to-bottom, we won't even know what to tell to the home office to look for, and you know it. Jesus Christmas, I'm sick of that mask of righteousness you wear on top of that squirming mass of chicken-hearted slug guts you call a soul. You want to cut bait? Have the bleedin' stones to say so. I vote we go, and I'm not afraid to admit it. We're bust here, and I don't want to spend the next fifty years working on no dead end. Let the robots do the grunt work and let the mission gods parse the data. No reason we can't be back on the way home by next week, and sitting on a beach in the Bahamas in three weeks subjective."

At mention of the Bahamas, a wave of homesickness swept over the room. Galbraith—Dar—let it continue and burn itself out, until we all were sitting in silence once again, the shame thick like clouds between us. Everyone wanted to go home. We all admitted it out loud.

And, though most of them couldn't tell for sure, it was written on everyone's face that just admitting to that desire made it repugnant. It is one thing, perhaps, to entertain cowardice in your own head. It is another to hear your thoughts spoken aloud by your enemy, or your colleague, and realize that she shares them. When it is stripped of the self-justification, and you see it for what it is. For what I saw mine as: The mewling of coddled children playing at explorer.

Dar was right. We were being ridiculous.

Well, if we were being ridiculous, I might as well be the one to own up. I had less prestige on the line than they did. I am, after all, just the tag-along.

"I know I am just the chronicler, however...but...look. Stella. What would happen if we chose Thorndale's second option? Seed our own flora and fauna alongside. Would there be a chance the plants could even grow?"

"Theoretically?"

"Best guess?"

"Assuming we can actually grow our plants in their soil without replacing all the bacteria...it's possible. I mean, there's native alleopathy to get around too, I'm sure, but it's been done before—getting around it, I mean. It'd be a long process. A lot of careful selection. We could be here for another century or two. The plants won't be in danger of poisoning from eating the native flora and fauna, unless we plant carnivores. It's the animals I'm not sure about. We might need to re-engineer them for aversion to certain plants, or...damn, what's the word? Christiana—when you monkey with persistent conditioned behavior?"

"Cultural seeding."

"Right. We might need to do cultural seeding just to give the mammals and birds a fighting chance. But, I mean, yeah, it might work. It's at least not crazy."

Hal rolled his eyes. "It *is* crazy. Best case your left-handed life won't know what your right-handed life is doing. What happens when these things start evolving? In a magnetosphere like this one—correct me if I'm wrong, Thorny—we're gonna see a whole different rate of mutations. Sooner or later, one of those mutations will let one of our little invasive species prey on the native biosphere. Or it'll allow one of their native species to eat ours up..."

I interrupted him: "Isn't that what a healthy integration looks like?"

"That's not the point. The point is that we're talking about separate sandboxes, and if you put two species next to each other long enough, there are no separate sandboxes. From a human point of view, we don't know what that'll do to our habitability when our plants and animals start adapting to the native biosphere."

"Smart guy. I like smart guys. The world needs more of 'em, don't you think?" Dar's grin looked positively predatory. "Animals adapting to the native biosphere could happen all on its own, so why *not* follow Jonathan's idea, and figure out how to do it preemptively."

"Absolutely out of the question!"

Discovery

A splash of glitter across a black velvet drape. The universe blinked back on.

Upon the drape, a marble.

And near the marble, a pebble. Red and purple and blue.

And soon, around the pebble, a single grain of salt, too small to detect.

Until it flashed.

It winked like a lighthouse beacon, flashing up from below.

Drawing towards it anything once contained within the human mind that might happen by.

Chapter 6
Continuity

THE FOUNDATION HAD CAREFULLY structured its program, leading its candidates through a particular obstacle course, providing them all appropriate information in exactly the right order, to prepare them for the second-to-last week.

Decision week.

The week when the mission gods decided the final teams.

The week when the candidates decided whether they were in or out.

The week when everyone was forced, finally, to confront their own impending mortality.

For this last, they worked in small groups with mentors who had been through a transition cycle before. The mentors did not walk them through the scientific or engineering aspects of resurrection. That information, strictly speaking, wasn't necessary.

"...the Greeks posited a world above our world which contained a perfect example of everything—the perfect chair, the perfect cube, the perfect lion, et cetera—and envisaged our world as the fallen world of matter, doomed always to fall short of the ideal, to wallow in corruption and impurity. That example, they called it an 'essence.' It is that which is *essential*."

Monk, the facilitator, drew a breath and perched herself on the edge of the table she'd previously been using as a podium. Her round, open face twitched the barest hint of a smile, and she continued in her rolling alto:

"Almost three thousand years ago, and they stumbled on something that it would take the rest of the world all that time to prove: Matter doesn't matter. Information is king. You are not made of the same stuff you were when you were born. It is statistically likely that not a single atom in your body is the same as the atoms you were born with."

"Monk?"

"Yes Xiyi."

"There is, I think, a problem."

"What's that?"

"If you take a ship, or an old ground car, and you make many of them from the same plans, and you use the same materials—even identical materials from the same sources—you will not have the same car. You will have two different cars. There will still be some differences."

"Would you? What if you were able to control everything, down to the spin of the subatomic particles? What if it was precisely identical..."

"But the particles would still be different particles. Isn't that the point of the Pauli Exclusion Principle?"

"It's...more involved than that, but let's ignore that for a moment. Pretend it's unimportant—a lot of philosophers argue just that. What would distinguish them?"

"Well..." Xiyi stumbled. Nobody else in the circle stepped up.

"Who are you?"

"Excuse me?"

"You, Chan Xiyi Aya, who are you?"

"I'm me."

"But what is that?"

"I am...a woman? A daughter? I suppose a not very good one. A writer. I write novels..."

"Go on."

"Well, I suppose...I climb. I am a tourist, I like traveling everywhere. I am an Asian Revivalist, and I spent a couple years helping to rebuild Shanghai. I got my master's degree in intra-system commercial law and I work for the Foundation in interjurisdictional compliance resolution." She wondered what else. What was important about who she was. Well, she knew one thing, at least, that set her apart from most people, but it wasn't as if she could talk about it openly.

But then again, why not? It was not as if it was anything that would threaten anyone. It was not as if it was possible for her to have any secrets here from anyone that would matter a week from now. Anyone that wound up on her team would find out everything about her anyway, and the mission gods surely knew, and anyone that didn't wind up on her team would spend the next several decades on a different planet. Monk still looked expectant. "When I was on my first Martian flight, I discovered a taste for gasping."

The admission drew a sharp collective breath from the group.

"Continue." Something in Monk's intent, open face seemed to expect this turn in the conversation. Even to welcome it. Xiyi blinked at the permission, and again at her own eagerness to relate.

"We had six of us in the shuttle, and what else are you to

doing when you are on the slow-boat? I had heard about it, and we had all that time to kill. Everyone who goes up gets put in the blood bugs, so it's not dangerous, not really. Not if you keep it under half an hour. But it feels like it.

"The first time was with the man in the stateroom across the passage. We wanted somewhere private, so we went into the airlock on our deck." Heat sped to her thighs with the memory, and Xiyi shifted in her seat. "They had the gel-packs there, the kinds you use for skin EVA? Well, I had heard about gasping, always wanted to try. He was game..." She closed her eyes and tried to concentrate on her words, to make her English clearer than normal. It seemed important.

"The inhalers, the polymer sealant for your lungs, they taste like bananas. And the goggles and ear plugs, they make it all like feeling in a circus. You think how ridiculous you must look, naked with goggles.

"Then you're pushing that void button and holding on. Your lungs gripping around nothingness, trying hard to breathe while you fill your lover's mouth with your own. You keep your lips locked together to preserve moisture, or you keep your mouths shut. You grip him with your legs to keep him inside, and you both move as fast, as hard, as desperate as you can. And when you come, you see the stars out the airlock door, nothing between you and the universe outside. And you try to stay conscious long enough to press the cycle button. It was the most intense...the most divine...I had ever experienced.

"Our neighbors down the hall heard the airlock. They wanted to know what happened, why it did, every detail. Keeping quiet...well, we tried, yes? We tried but could not. Then, after we confessed that night, they joined us.

"On our last approach to Mars, before we entered orbit, we climbed into a cargo net, the all four of us, tethered to the ship, and had it out in the naked void…" Xiyi ran out of words, remembering the terror and panic and glory of the moment. "Have you ever looked at death and seen the whole universe at once? Had creation and destruction meet in your own body at the center of the universe? I…I…" She suddenly realized again where she was, and blushed. "I guess that is who I am. I am the woman who finds such adventures. And embraces them."

Monk smiled, which Xiyi only saw because she dared a peek up from the floor. Her peers were silent, and she did not dare look at them. She asked Xiyi:

"So if you were to do that again, would it be the same?"

"No. I mean…it might be better. It may be worse. It may just be different. But it would not be the same."

"Why?"

"I am a different person now."

"How?"

"I…well, I am older. It would not be new…"

"So, experience? That makes the difference?"

"Yes."

Monk nodded, as if Xiyi had just proved her point, though Xiyi was still not sure what it was.

The instructor's attention seemed to pull back, no longer focused on Xiyi, but encompassing the whole group again. "Anytime we find a way to enhance, extend, or modify life, or transfer consciousness, or alter our perception, these arguments rise to the surface. Different cultures have reached different solutions to the question of identity—'what makes me, me?' What we've discovered is that the only irreducible part of a being, the only truly unique thing, is the continuity. We are all nexuses of changing patterns of information. Our ability to maintain identity depends on our continuity with our past selves, and our future selves. This is the guiding principle of the laws that govern the way we work with consciousness.

"For example, you've all known someone who did a Nirvana. Do you know why it takes six months, when we can do a medical backup in a few hours?"

Another woman in the circle, one that Xiyi would later come to know as Dr. Christiana Sansa, said: "Acute upload is a serious felony."

"Ah," said Monk, "but why?"

She replied: "Because the functioning of the mind is dependent upon and modified by biological processes. An acute transfer leaves a mind helpless and grasping. It goes insane, like a full-body case of phantom limb. Instead of heaven, they've transferred themselves into hell, and they make the etherspace hell for the other residents."

"Good functional reasons. But what is the principle underneath it?"

"Continuity and consanguinity."

"Exactly. At any given point, the continuity of experience OR the consanguinity of the platform—that's the identical physical state of the body," Monk added to alleviate the perplexed looks she got from a couple of the trainees, "must be preserved. Consanguinity ensures that the consciousness operates as it would have on its accustomed platform. Continuity gives a traceable history. Remove either one of these, and you risk damaging the person. Remove both at once, and the being you re-create is not the being you destroyed, it is only a copy."

OVER THE NEXT SEVERAL days, Monk fielded some more questions, and ran through some more exercises. She seemed intent on making sure that each of them understood.

By the end of the week, they did.

"Before we go into teams and you get briefed on the planets you'll each be going to, there's one last item we need to cover, and I've set aside the rest of our day to work through it.

"Now, in order to work, our method preserves continuity at the expense of consanguinity. This means that in order to go, your body will have to die. You'll be uploaded at this end as close to death as we can manage. Then, your consciousness will be stored statically—you will experience nothing different than if you went under anesthesia for surgery.

"At the other end, your body will be cloned and force-grown to your present physical age, then your consciousness will be written to it, and you will come out of the coma. You'll require physical therapy for the first several weeks, to retrain and strengthen your new muscles, but otherwise, you'll feel just like you do now. Any modifications you undertake at that point are, of course, your own business. Normal medical facilities are being built on-site as we speak, and will be ready for you when you arrive."

She was right. It did take all day.

Throughout, Xiyi held her tongue. The question she had was not one that would put her classmates at ease about her character, at least judging by their reaction to her gasping tale. She determined to talk to Monk after the others had dispersed.

Christiana Sansa evidently had the same idea, so Xiyi waited at the back like a misbehaving schoolgirl waiting to see the principal. The small, well-padded institutional comfort around her didn't quell the quavering excitement and dread in the pit of her stomach. The disappointment of not being able to experience the trip itself had melted in the blaze of a lightning bolt striking so close to her most private pit of shame, that part of her incurably fixated on a fall from a tree when she was four years old, and the unbearable exhilaration, surviving even the months of recovery that followed. That unaccountable feeling of being extra-alive, as if she had tapped straight into the universe's vital force.

"Xiyi?" Christiana waved a hand in front of her face.

Xiyi started. "What? Yes? Can I help you?"

"She's all yours," she waved at Monk, then started to walk away, then stopped. "Oh, after you're done, we should talk."

Xiyi didn't know why Christiana should think they needed to talk—they'd only first met this cycle—but considering the kinds of things that people had shared in the group this cycle, considering the kinds of things *she'd* shared this cycle, she was not at all certain that it was a conversation she wanted to have.

"Monk?"

Monk looked up from her handheld, smiled kindly and stowed the device in a pocket of her billowing overcoat. "Xiyi, what can I do for you?"

"Well. I...I have found myself wondering...unusually..."

"Yes?"

"Do...um...do we, uh, get to choose how we die?"

Monk slid down into her chair so she could be eye-to-eye with Xiyi, rather than looking down at her. It was a gesture Xiyi had learned to appreciate, the way Monk always met the trainees at eye level.

"I just have always...well...wondered what it would feel like. The shooting. To be shot, I mean. With a gun. And to be able to experience that, and remember that, without the disabling...having to be disabled...yes, disabled by it...one does not get such chances very frequently, does one?"

"I suppose one doesn't. We couldn't shoot you in the head—you wouldn't remember it, and you wouldn't survive for upload."

"What of the heart? There would maybe time enough? I...would perhaps you speak to the mission gods about the matter?"

She promised she would. Xiyi walked out of the room on weak knees, where she found Christiana Sansa leaning with her back and left foot pressed against the wall, her dye-crimson close-cropped hair pressing against the wall making a crown of spikes around her head, and humming to herself.

"Get what you need, luv?"

"I think so, yes."

Christiana pushed off the wall, began walking. Xiyi fell into step with her. "They posed the teams this morning, you hear 'bout it?"

"What? I thought they did not post those until tomorrow."

"Sure'n that's what they said, but some old bugger posted it today."

"Oh. Very well, then. I guess I need to look..."

"That's why I needed to talk to you, I did."

"What? We are teammates?"

"We are. I'm the Chief Cladistics Officer."

"Oh! Pleased to meet you. It will be good to have along a friend."

"That's...what I wanted to slip you. There's no easy way to break it, but better you knowin' now than finding out the hard way at the other end. Another one of your friends is coming along, too, seems."

"Who?"

"Darren Galbraith."

"Dar? How..."

"He's Mission Commander."

XIYI FOUND DAR IN their customary spot in the med

center, already stripped and laying naked on the table, his torso propped up on his elbows, his nose pointed at his handheld, his eyes scanning a book.

"Kali Choot Ke Safaid Jhaat!." She whapped the handheld out from under his eyes, sending it clattering harmlessly against the far wall.

"What?"

"You said you were one of us."

"One of what?"

"Normals. Neurotypicals..."

"I never said.."

"...and you're a goddamned *psychopath*!"

"And? So?"

"You lied to me!"

"I did..."

"You liar. Make me trust you, twist me to..."

"Wait, hold on, kiddo. Settle down. First, I didn't lie, I just didn't volunteer the truth. Second, if I did lie...have you *looked* at the mission rationale for psychopaths? Have you read the profile? Lying and manipulation are part of the job. Third, I hang out with you because we have fun together, I don't owe you a thing. And fourth, you'd better just get your ass used to listening to me and trusting my word since you're on my team and what I say on that planet goes."

Xiyi smoldered, then found he had given her an immense latitude, and calmed down. "I suppose, when we get there, I guess we will be have to professionals."

"Exactly."

"And we leave next week."

"That's the plan."

"Fine."

"We have an understanding, then?"

"In that case, I suppose..." She swung her bag and clocked him full on the side of the head.

He howled, and tried to curl around his damaged, bleeding cranium, and fell onto the floor.

Xiyi left him there for the mission gods to find. Maybe they'd get there before he bled into his brain.

But she kind of hoped they didn't.

Courtship

From bounded jump to endless fall, a forever-descent to a goal so unrealistic, so chancy, that, scant years before, no one would have believed it.

With small pushes this way and that, limited fuel expenses, the ship nudged itself into the groove, riding the rimline to the rendezvous with its mate.

The two vessels met, locking their collars together, sharing coordinates, spinning up generators for the next stage.

The ship ejected its cargo. The capsule fired its braking thrusters and dropped out of the sky.

Thick and hot, the air wrapped around it, until tongues of flame leapt from its feet, settling it down with perfect precision onto the prepared surface of planet Filbert.

And then, the robots woke up.

Chapter 7

Plans

Expedition: Filbert
Mission Day 239
Mission Historian Personal Perspective
Year 2253 of the Common Era

CONTINUING FROM MY PREVIOUS summary entry, retrospective to the First Planetary Summit on mission day fifty-five...

Thorndale might not have been in command, but he could out-shout Darren Galbraith like an elephant out-shouts a shrew. "I'm not joking, Darren. We are NOT talking about this."

Our virologist, Hannah Kaimakli—Kaima—nodded urgently at the screen, made the ASD signal for 'emergency'. "Take it off the board, Xiyi."

"If you continue in this manner I will be forced to invoke Section Forty-Six." Thorndale remained standing.

"Xiyi, take it off the board! Now!"

Dar shouted over both of them: "Shut up the pair of you, and you," he aimed his eyes at me as if he could burn me down by blinking, "take your hands off that console and get over here."

I kept my fingers on the console. "We're not refactoring

the colonists, Dar."

"Agreed," Thorndale said.

"Oh? Why's that?"

"Because you're never going to get colonists to agree to it," Kaima's condescension seemed to coat the room, "And because you're violating every law and ethical protocol governing the continuity of personhood, and because...goddammit, because it's repellent. I can't believe we're even talking about this."

"We're not talking about this," Thorndale growled, "If you've all had quite enough, under section..."

"Do you see a legislative body? A king?" Dar stood up and waved at the empty air. "We have the mission law, Kaima, and that's about it, and mission law doesn't say a bloody thing about this kind of thing, because nobody's ever been here before." He pointed at Thorndale. "That means you don't have grounds to unseat me, your invocation is even more full of shit than you are." He took a breath, brought his volume down a couple notches. He held his arms bent at the elbows, as if he were carrying a serving tray. "Look, folks, this is new ground. We're on our own out here. We're making this up as we go along..."

"If someone comes out of that incubator different than they went in at the other end, you've violated their fundamental human rights!" Prescott thundered.

Kaima was right on his heels. "Change a single piece of the protein sequence of a dormant germ line and you change the expression, that's bad enough..."

"Why?" Dar said. "Grav monkeys have been around for centuries..."

"Which is completely beside the point. That's modification pre-implantation, or it's a long voluntary process by *one* conscious, continuous being. You're not sentencing one being to be a slave to the memories of another. Consciousness emerges from the body that carries it. To move that consciousness to a different body, you have to supply all the same inputs. You have to supply a near-perfect copy of that same body..."

"We modify our bodies all the time. What's the..."

Christiana's caramel cockney broke in, a thick quiet, like an orchestral swell, that dampened the cacophony. I realized, again, how grateful I was to have her along. "The difference, Darren dear, is that all those other processes are ones we do while consciousness is active. We even do Nirvana uploads incrementally, starting with the neural prosthesis to wean the consciousness off the biological substrate gradually so that continuity is maintained."

"Continuity, continuity, Christ, why are you all so hung up on continuity?"

"Because continuity is *all we are*. Jesus, your first doctorate is in consciousness theory, you know this."

"And theories change."

"Dammit, this is 101 level stuff. This ain't something you could do after they came out, have 'em take a mod. You're talking about *rearranging the entire metabolism*. You can't transition that. You'll be creating a race from scratch and burdening them with the identities of people who you're cheating of life. We don't know what a metabolic hand-switch will do to brain function and personality. I mean, Christ, Darren, I know you're a psychopath, but holy shit."

I gave up and left the console, heading for the circle where I could actually participate. "Is what you are speaking of even possible? Jonathan, more this your area, right? And you did raise the topic..."

He nodded. "Theoretically, yeah, it's possible. I'd need a few months, maybe a few years, to build some proxy animals and run some tests, but I'm pretty sure I could do it."

"I absolutely forbid it," Thondale said.

Kaima joined him: "Squared."

Hal and Stella cubed it.

Dar laughed. A genuine, crippling belly-laugh. "You're not in command here. I haven't given any illegal orders. Okay, so you forbid it, and you say it can be done, and you don't like it, and you think it's repellent. I get it. I'm not an idiot. So let's table it for now. What other options do we have?"

Since I was unofficial secretary anyway, I looked up at the board. "Number one: Raze the biosphere."

Nobody seemed very excited about it. Some back and forth flew, but Stella closed the discussion out when she said: "Look, leave aside for a minute the problem of whether or not there are sentients here we ain't found yet, maybe hiding on another continent or an island or some other place where we haven't done deep survey work. Forget that we'd be ruining, instead of just modifying, their entire future. Forget *everything* we'd have to do to make sure it's actually legal to flash-fry this place and start over from scratch.

"Razing this biosphere *is not* just a matter of driving some species to extinction. We're talking about a whole unique form of life that's never even been observed before. I don't have to tell all of you what that could mean—how much we don't know about what that could mean—for our understanding of how the universe works. That's worth more than just the planet."

"Alright," Dar nodded, "You've sold me. Better to leave this place here as a preserve and go home. And," he studied the board for a second, "I think it's safe to assume that if we can't raze the planet, we shouldn't raze a whole continent for a foothold, either. We don't know how the web works here, or what it'll do to the climate, and that kind of depth would take a century or so to work out—assuming I'm not overestimating?" He looked at Thorndale, sitting in a cloud of indignation. "Thorny? You're the ecologist."

"Hm? What? Oh! Yes, that's about right." And then, as an afterthought: "Might take a bit longer."

"Okay. Xiyi, knock that one off the screen, will you?"

I obliged, then read out: "Next live option: establish domed cities, like on Ceres or Ganymede."

"I don't think we need to argue this one, we know how that one goes," Dar said, "The mission gods won't be happy with it, but we know how to do it. Leave that one up."

"Very well," I said. "Next, set up an automated deep-survey for the whole planet and leave it to run. We get out of here, go home."

"Or they send us back out to staff another expedition. There might be no magical piña coladas in our future," grumbled Thorndale.

Kaima folded her arms. "They can't do that..."

"Read your contract," Dar said, "They can. They have the option."

"I know I'm just the chronicler here, but this seems like to me the best one. We all are chasing around the tree of not enough knowledge, and this is one, the only scheme that will give us the information we need. We will not get to see the implementation, yes, but we will have advanced the mission. It seems to me worth at least considering."

Thorndale shrugged "Dovetails with redesigning the survey protocol..."

"Actually, I reckon there's another little wrinkle with that little 'nalysis of yours," Hal said. "We just scratched the surface here and found a world like nothin' we ever expected. If we're gonna recommend a redesign in the way the Foundation does its surveys, we'd better stick here and find out what other nasty 'boos' this place has all saved up for us. One way or the tuther, this ain't the cakewalk we loaded up for. We're looking at a fair few decades 'stead of a few years."

"We're going to need to start thinking about regen schedules, and continuity," Stella said.

"Wait, hold on," Kaima said. "Continuity? As in children?"

"As in."

"I did *not* sign up to be a brood mare!"

"Ladies!" Dar snapped, "Enough. Okay, here's what happens. We *will* collect all the data we can get our hands on to redesign the survey protocol. I want six teams building the equipment to go and survey the other continents in-depth. That means Thorny, you're putting together a knock list for the first pass. Jonathan, your first priority is getting your tech monkeys to coordinate with Thorny's people and make sure that they design and build the equipment to pull this off. Christiana, Hal, Stella, everyone else, I want a list of the things you need to know about. We're going to need to rig some nanosats to bounce communications around.

"Now, everyone who's left, which includes all of you—no department heads, in fact, no one in this room, leaves the compound for the survey. No exceptions. You understand?"

Dar paused to let a wave of grumbles subside, including mine. The idea of being able to get out and really see the world tugged at me like a winter vista in the Alps.

"Wait, I thought you were all professionals, what kind of crap is this? What am I gonna do if you all fall off the chopper or get eaten by a swamp monster, huh? I'll have to restart you from backups, and then bring you all the way up to speed, and re-integrate you, and the survivors will treat you like a zombie, and some of you would be pissed to find out that I'd done that cause you believe that it would damage your soul or that you'd be some kind of monster or that I'd imposed your sins on someone who is effectively your child or some kinda shit like that. So, you'd be dead, and your relationships ruined, and the mission would get completely screwed over." He looked straight at Christiana. "See, I do pay attention. So, anyway...

"Like I was saying. Everyone who's left, which includes all of you, gets to work on the other two live plans. I want survey teams sending out expeditions to map the optimal placement for domed cities. Oh, and one more thing. We *will be* keeping Jonathan's idea on the table, and you're all at his disposal. Jonathan, clone me some freaks and figure out what it'll take to adapt human biology to this planet. Figure out if we can do it as a mod, or if we have to go the Grav Monkey route. Mods are better.

"Okay. That's it." He looked at me. "Recording's on the server?"

"It does that automatically," I said.

"Good. I want answers, people. Let's get moving."

That is how we got started down this path. The last few months here have taught me many things, chief among them that I never really appreciated my life before I died. Please, do not misunderstand. I enjoyed my life as much as anybody, but despite all the adventures, and the work most people would call meaningful, I never quite felt as if I owned my time. Risks, I found exciting, but I never much worried what would happen if they went wrong. I had friends and family, but they did not anchor me. I suppose I would not have come on this junket if they had.

But sunsets on this planet, with their sharp white-yellow burning out to orange, and the dazzling deep purple of the vegetation, and the hazy, endless canyon below us bursting with life...they are enough to make even the hardest, most stony heart melt like wax and fall in love with life, as if for the first time.

There are many evenings in which I watch it from the fence line, but I have found in recent weeks a stand of juniper behind the shop dome that allowed me to gain purchase on the antenna guy-wires and climb to the top. From up there, I can see everything for at least a hundred kilometers. It made the sunsets endless.

I had, so far, kept the secret, and climbed up there only to watch the sunset, and only when I was sure I couldn't be seen, so I would have a place that nobody would molest me, least of all Dar and his interminable badgeration. And that night, after the meeting where Dar pronounced his plans from on high to the consternation of every person there, I was shaking all the way from my toes to my nose.

Relief? Yes. A lot of relief. This was planet worth preserving. Raze the biosphere? I gave Dar a lot of credit for that one. He was not under an obligation to knock it out of the running like that. It was a valid interpretation of our mission parameters, so far as I could tell. But to think of the purple valley before me as green—or worse, barren—it felt as if someone were taking a razor blade and nicking at my heart just to see how much it could take before it split open and spilled my blood into places I could never use it.

Longing, too. Not for home, but for more people. It is a lonely thing, being the only normal person in a sea of dysfunctional genius. As much as I have come to love and tolerate and even enjoy my friends here, it feels as if I am the one Mandarin speaker in a room full of people speaking Cantonese. Everything is just different enough that I feel permanently out of joint.

But that sunset...

Looking out from up on that dome makes everything worth it. It is the closest I will ever be to what most people here call "God." The universe truly is the sonata that generates its own orchestra. Up there. I hear only the music.

Usually.

"It's not going to work." Dar's voice nearly scared me out of my skin.

I pressed my hands flat down onto the dome's smooth surface, so that I didn't start sliding. I clung to my temper so that it didn't fly away from me either. "Dar, go away."

"We need to talk."

"Never in all my time on this planet have I found myself in need of hearing you talk." I did not turn to face him. If I did not actually see him with my eyes, he would not truly be intruding on my evening.

"Okay, then, I need to speak with you."

"Later." There was a chill on the breeze. I pulled my shawl up around my shoulders.

"Can't wait."

"Find a toilet if holding it in is too much."

"Goddammit, Xiyi. I have to *talk* with you."

"Whyever, for fuck's sake, Dar?"

"Because I owe you an apology. For before, back in indoctrination."

I do not think there are any other words I could have heard that I would have expected less. Or that I would have believed less. I am not sure whether I said nothing out of shock, or out of scorn. Either way, he was not willing to wait.

"I'm sorry," he said. "I really am."

My eyes rolled without my consent. "No, you're not."

"Okay, I'm not. But it's what I'm expected to say." He was moving closer. Standing perhaps a meter behind me on my left.

"Then say it again, and make me believe it."

"I'm sorry that I misled you. I'm sorry that it hurt you. I won't pretend I feel guilty, but I do miss being your friend."

"Hmph." I actually wanted to believe him, and that shocked me. Like walking into the bathroom to find your father brushing his teeth naked. "Do you really? Or do you just need me now, so it is convenient to let me think so?"

"I really do. We do have feelings, you know. They just don't quite work the same way."

"So? Explain."

"Ha. That would be like trying to explain what it's like to be a man. Since I've never been anything else, I don't have the slightest clue." He sat down beside me. I kept my eyes on the retreating day. "The textbooks say that you have a hard time disconnecting your feelings, while I have to have a reason to connect mine up. They say that you can get pleasure out of things that bore me to death. And they say that you can feel guilty about things that just happen."

"And you can't?"

He shrugged. "I never really wanted to. Seems like a waste of time. I do know that I miss you. I love your crazy way of thinking, the way everything matters to you. You were always loads of fun."

"Why is that?"

"Well, you're always...interesting. That's hard to do

without. When I heard they'd put you on my team...well, I don't think I've ever been happier. And I sure as taxes never got more pissed than when you knocked my head in like that. So, like I said..." His voice had changed. I turned my head and found him looking at me, as if...well, as if. "...I'm sorry. For what it's worth. I miss you."

And I kissed him. As well as I knew his body, I'd never tasted him before. We had never had that kind of a friendship. He tasted sweet, the way lies do.

I managed to catch my breath, find some words. "What are you doing?"

"You kissed me. I just came to talk."

"Oh, right." I rearranged myself. "What about...I mean...what did you want to..."

"Oh. The plan. This isn't going to work."

"It seemed fine."

"Well, maybe. I think I'm going to get some trouble from Thorny."

"And you want me for to do what?"

"Keep me in the loop..."

"Dar, I can't do that. My job..."

"Keep me in the loop. That's an order."

"Give me a good reason."

"Because I'm mission..."

"I said a *good* reason."

"Okay, fine."

And that time, he kissed me, and I felt like every organ was made of glass like to splinter at just the right frequency. He didn't let me up for air. That was okay, though. I didn't let him up either. But we did lose most of our clothes up there, sliding down the dome while we gasped and muscled our way to a treaty in that last bit of sunset.

I remember thinking, at the time, how much different his body felt without all the scars accumulated from a lifetime of living in it. As if it were all, somehow, not quite real. A dream. The kind of dream that you never want to wake up from.

Until the time is much, much too late.

Resurrection

Like spools of yarn, curling up into discrete piles, untwisted for braiding on a loom. That one a pair of Ls, this one a pair of Xs.

This string for a nucleus, that one for expression, a third one for mitochondria, a fourth for the messengers.

Muscle, bone, fiber, sinew, skin, the self-made manifestation of the yarn that weaves itself.

Purpose, self-guiding, held back only by the restriction: Thou shalt not wake.

And, bit by bit, a body grew.

Chapter 8

Last Breath of The Promised Land

OUT OF THE SOUTH CHINA SEA, like flesh and skin, a living city grew on the steel-and-concrete skeleton left over from the Asiatic War. The first ever living city, rebuilt while the rest of the mainland baked in the radiation left over from the ICBMs, its buildings made strong and flexible by vines and moss designed to generate their own power, their own oxygen. It rose from the ashes of nuclear war like a forest from the aftermath of a fire.

Hong Kong, city of life. Stage one of the Pan-Asian revival project. Xiyi had been here before, once, during her training before her team went to seed the same changes in Shanghai. With buildings stretching like phototropes up into the sky, its mosses seeding its clouds with salt mist, its trusses and drain spouts delivering pure water to the people who lived in her, she was a prototype for a new world.

Her parents lived in the Xang Ho One, one of the newer buildings around the harbor. This morning, she had left the Foundation's indoctrination center in San Diego and taken the

Undersea to the tube port in Kagoshima, then hopped across on the Feather Express. She took lunch in the street market near her parents' building, to quiet the anticipation in her stomach, then walked the fondly-remembered streets before finally reaching an understanding with her unease, and circling back to her parents' tower.

They knew she was coming. She'd told them she had big news that would make them proud. Even with all they'd done before, she figured that she owed them that much. She tapped the door with trembling fingers, and it opened to the inscrutable Indian face of her father. Vapors of oyster sauce and sesame oil flooded out past him to tempt her inside. She kissed him, as she was obliged, and her heart fell as she found no warmth in his perfunctory affection, turning her stomach sour.

Inside, her mother and sister prepared a feast.

She greeted them. She almost did not hear her own words.

They seemed not to either. It took a full moment for Mims, her mother, to say in mish-mash Mandarin "Get the broccoli, we are almost out of time."

Xiyi had to mentally translate it, having always learned the native tongue of her locale instead of the ever-changing pidgin that dominated the home. This was by design—the both of them had refused to speak to her in their Panglish lingua franca, believing it would cripple her ability to communicate with her peers. They spoke to her only in broken versions of the local tongue.

"Out of time?" Xiyi's Mandarin, on the other hand, was as pitch-perfect as a non-native ever gets.

"Your brother, he is coming."

"With Lilly?" Xiyi stashed her bag, bursting with legacies from her soon-to-end life, neatly in the closet. She normally would have brought only a wallet, but she wanted to leave some favorite trinkets in the care of her family, to show them that she still honored them even in her trek to the edge of the universe.

"Yes. She is ripe and beautiful now. Have you seen the pictures?"

Xiyi bristled, then stuffed the feeling down. It had been ten years since that fight about her career, everyone had forgiven each other. They understood why she'd chosen the path she had, and she understood why it frightened them. Her time in Shanghai had proved her right. They'd moved to Hong Kong from the refugee center in Morocco, because of what she told them about her time here. They could not still seriously disapprove. It was just the paranoia of old pain plaguing her now.

The broccoli gave way beneath the knife. Stiff crackles, the sound of the only part of her childhood she loved. She passed them to her sister Adi, but Mims insisted on inspecting them. Finding Xiyi's knifework inadequate to the glorious nature of the occasion, she chucked the veggies in the bin and snatched the knife away from Xiyi, and muttered how stupid she was that she could not get such a simple thing right, and began afresh with another bunch.

"If you do not do this well, what you can expect to make use of you?" Broken English now. Her most condescending mode of engagement.

"I...I am going on a geosurvey. Out past the Mannix limit. We are making a new world."

"Fool." Mims grunted.

Adi clucked her tongue in a "now you've done it" sort of way.

"I did not hear you, Mims?"

"That is very nice, Xi, but where will you meet a good man on such a planet?"

Xiyi didn't know how to respond. The doorbell interrupted her anyway, and her father once again shuffled to the threshold and threw it open, this time revealing her brother Kabr and his French wife Lilly.

"Ah! They are here!" Broken French this time. Better than her English. To honor the pregnant Lilly. Mims left her kitchen and doddered to the door to extend the honor of the household. "Please forgive that we are so unprepared to receive you. Xiyi has thrown off our entire schedule." Mims took Lilly's face in her hands and kissed the air near her cheeks, as the French do. She then looked down at the near-term belly. "May..."

"Of course." Lilly was glowing. Near bursting with life and pride. She guided Mims's hands to the thin membrane surrounding the baby, and Mims muttered a blessing in her native Nepalese. "You see, Xi, how beautiful?" Now in Mandarin, so Lilly would not understand. "How she has made sure the family will live on and survive your selfishness?"

Adi clucked her tongue again. Quiet enough so that only Xi could hear. Little clicks. Like darts, coated in curare.

"I am certain," Xiyi said in the iciest Mandarin she could manage, "she will fail somehow to die in childbirth."

Mims's mouth fell open in horror. Xiyi stalked to the closet, threw open the door, dove for her bag, and shoved her way through the crowded entryway. She tramped down the hall to the lift, took it to the street, and stalked to the waterfront.

She remembered the city smelling like rain. That was before her parents moved here. Now, it just smelled like death to her.

She thought they'd be proud of her, making a new world.

More the fool, her. Mims was right, about that part at least.

She left her bag in a tide pool. A gift to the anemones of long-treasured books and childhood mementos.

Hong Kong fell behind her plane like a diseased thing, all life and decay and dishonor and death, and she closed her eyes and brought to mind the image of the drive ship that, very soon, would be her forever-home.

Revival

All at once, the city lights blinked on. They glowed green under the watchful robotic eye. The layout corresponded exactly to the map stored in its memory banks.

Error check at 10^{-30}. Green light.

Its probes pierced the spinal column at the base of the skull. Cradled in the machine's arms, the priority eight patient—subject number thirty-six—jolted awake.

Xiyi saw the white dome stretching above her head, a blank sheet of panic filled with all the terrors her reptilian brain could muster. Then, registering her distress, the mechanical nurse flooded her system with probes, uptaking the excess cortisol, stimulating her seratonin receptors.

Her noisy mind mellowed. Its stimulus gates lowered. It accepted what its senses told it. Xiyi, not knowing what to expect, observed it all as if from a distance. The dome lit up. Pictures scrolled past. Figures. Letters. None of it made much sense, but at first it didn't need to. It just needed to be. Just as the electrical shocks pulsing in her muscles needed to be. She didn't know why they needed to be. They just did.

Eternities later—504 hours, according to the robot—she remembered her name. Then, she remembered the bullet, and wished she hadn't. Some curiosities were not meant to be indulged.

Bit by bit, as if in a trickle, her life came back to her. The details of her decision. Eventually the notion that she'd been successful occurred to her, and she wondered if the rest of the team had survived. Or if the spare personal baggage she'd been allowed had made it through the landing.

Somewhere around the 672nd hour, she realized that she'd remembered how to dream.

Chapter 9

Of All I Survey

Expedition: Filbert
Mission Day 240
Mission Historian Personal Perspective
Year 2253 of the Common Era

CONTINUING MY DISTILLATION OF my notes. So many notes. So much to account for. Waking up on day fifty-six, I felt his warmth against my skin.

I did not intend it, waking up next to Dar. Not that first day, not any of the hundred days after. I did not intend it, yet it happened. It felt somehow inevitable, like finding shelter from a snowstorm in a cave next to a hibernating bear.

But that is where I woke up. And it is where I stayed for the first half-hour that morning, studying his body, remembering where all the old scars had been, savoring the feeling of unreality that, since his resurrection on this new world, they no longer existed. That feeling allowed me to ignore, for a few minutes, the fact that reality had grown spines, and we were stuck on the sharp end of one. It reminded me that I had forgotten about my own scars, and how they did not persist through resurrection cycles, and what that meant.

I stayed at first, that morning, to savor. Later, I stayed in from habit, and for the comfort. Now I stay in every morning because my roommate, Stella Bosch, puttered about for the first hour ever morning, and I did not want her to see what I noticed this week: that I am gaining weight. In one place. Because my scars and surgeries, including that one my parents had gotten me at menarche, did not persist through my death. Because my new body functioned better than it was supposed to.

After she left. I slipped out of bed, leaving Dar behind me, sprawling across the bed as if I had never been there, owning it even in his sleep. I did not try to scrub away my stupidity this morning, there would have been no point. I was carrying it inside me now, and besides, no amount of scrubbing ever dampened the looks of betrayal and disgust I got from my friends who were incensed that I was sleeping with the enemy.

We have all chosen sides, they seemed to say, and you picked the wrong one.

Call it an alliance. I didn't realize we had one until that first time, but it had been growing. Uncomfortable and unacknowledged, but there all the same. The only two of the whole team who weren't "stables." Even though we had so little in common, that single fact conspired to drive us together.

But I still have my job, a job I must do, even in a fractured compound where every meeting is a shouting match and every hope of finishing the job has long since withered into bitterness. We are truly serving time in prison now, held here by Dar's iron word. He is determined that we finish the job, even at the cost of everyone's lives. They put psychopaths in leadership because they can more easily prioritize rules and ideas over desires or relationships. Empathy is a cruel saddle for the back of a king, or at least that's what the gods think.

We have already lost six of our original thirty-five-plus-one. Three of our six survey teams were lost—one due to weather, one due to equipment failure, and the third due to some kind of parasite that found a way to adapt itself to our biology. Too many to bear, and I am still numb. Details are in the official mission files.

So much of what happened this year were things we could not have intended.

But yes, I am supposed to provide a common person's view of what is happening here. What is happening is hell. Maybe worse than hell, because when you are in a real hell, you cannot ignore the situation you find yourself in. But here? Everyone seems numb. Resentment bubbles beneath the surface. What used to be professionalism punctuated by common purpose, even some affection, has all boiled away like water sublimated into a vacuum.

Jonathan bears the brunt of it. As head of molecular bioengineering, he is the person who must spearhead the work on retooling the metabolism. The resentment has only intensified since the most recent disaster with the expedition to the fourth continent. I didn't see him in mess this morning, which was not a big surprise. The place is a ghost town at the best of times, since everyone started eating separately. Sneaking in throughout the day, taking leftovers to reheat. It started as expedience when the workload exploded. Then it became habit. A good excuse to keep away from the grumbling. A good way to avoid enemies.

I took my breakfast to Jonathan's office. He has gained a lot of weight in the past few months, his face had gotten long and slack, like someone too accustomed to being drunk—all of it is the misery. We none of us have enough printer allowance to manufacture enough alcohol to do that to a person.

I found him slumped over his screen, paging through experimental results, agar plates stacked next to him a meter high. The third party to our unconscious alliance, driven to my team and Dar's by the hatred of the others in the colony. He hated us for it. I did not blame him. I hated Dar for the same reason, but it was too late to do anything about it now.

He looked even less happy than usual.

"What is troubling you?"

His face swung round toward me, utterly blank, like the face of some massive radio telescope without the decency to appear curious.

"What?" I asked.

After a moment, he leaned out around me as if to check for eavesdroppers, then said: "I found it. I got it working. Left-handed metabolism in a previously right-handed host."

"Wait, is that bad?"

"It ain't good."

"Why not?"

"Because," he gritted through clenched teeth, as if he thought I were an idiot, "Now I have to start working higher up the food chain, and people are gonna notice. We've got some grade-A true believers here, they're gonna burn us at the stake. Unless..."

"Unless what?"

"Unless you don't tell him."

Expedition: Filbert
Mission Day 272
Mission Historian Personal Perspective
Year 2253 of the Common Era

I DIDN'T TELL HIM. Not right away. Dying to come here was one thing—an incremental step beyond everything I'd ever known—retooling everything I was in order to stay here seemed like another thing entirely. I was on Dar's side because I thought we really should explore all our options. Filbert was worth it. More now, even, than it was before.

On my two hundred fifty-seventh day out of quarantine, Jonathan brought up at the staff meeting that he needed to go on an extended field expedition, just locally. He thought he was on to something that might make all of our conflict unnecessary, that might allow us to adapt to the biosphere without changing our metabolisms, and he wanted to examine more of the native biosphere to see if he could turn up the missing piece of the puzzle. He needed an assistant to go with him, but it couldn't be Jo, his regular assistant—she needed to stay here and continue the microbiology work on the other projects.

"No," he said, "it'll have to be Xiyi."

I was creeping up to my third month, far enough in that I was not going to be able to hide it from Dar much longer, so I was happy to go. And then, since I was on the mission roster, Geology handed me a GPR and spec sheet to do a detailed ground survey of the area down-canyon. Potential city dome sites, conforming to these specifications, with less than six degrees of grade, built on proper bedrock so that the danger of seismic or weather disturbance was minimal.

I put on a secondskin and got fitted for a face mask, climbed into the bright orange all-terrain camping buggy, and drove Jonathan out through the fence. He sat in the back and fussed with his figures, which was almost as good as going out alone.

Winter leaned on the world like an old redwood half-fallen-over. With the long days, Filbert's thermal inertia gave it forever-seasons. Autumns and springs that stretched long, summers that ran to swelter, and winters that dove deep. Its orbital period was actually shorter than Earth's, but its eclipse cycles with the Fred that hung heavy in the sky, and its hard axial inclination, shifted everything weather-like on the planet to the extreme. The original robotic survey had observed Filbert for a year, noted the slow change in seasons, and predicted a long, mild climatic cycle.

But, like a large building, Filbert was slow to lean and quick to topple. Its winter shift coincided with passing through the ecliptic in its orbital progression around the gas giant. Night combined with regular, long eclipses. Deep cold chased by rapid warming, as if we lived four days a week in the Antarctic, and three days in the tropics.

THE BUGGY CRUNCHED MERRILY along our three hundred mile loop. I spent my days working the GPR and the other toys they'd sent me with, walking among the dormant, stubborn trees, smelling the rich fruity ferment of a forest that never quite went to sleep, not even for winter. I cataloged a few hundred new species—my favorite sort I called Qi, after the spirit of life, because it, more than anything else, conveyed to me the spirit of this place.

It was large, about the size of a Shetland pony, had six legs—all the higher animals on Filbert seem to—and looked like a long-limbed wolverine covered in feathers. They come in five basic patterns, adapted to different niches, but mine had purple and black mottling on top of splotchy gray stripes.

I should say, I called her mine. She found me when I was running a GPR pass over a wide shelf overlooking the canyon. Only a stand of gnarled trees blocked my view back to the compound twenty klicks up the vale at the foot of the mountain. Because I was not underneath the canopy, I did not feel obliged to wear my face mask. There was not much risk of contact toxicity when not working in the close environment, so I saw no reason to deprive myself of the wondrous smells in this place.

You have never smelled smells like there are during the winter in Basecamp Canyon on Filbert. The animals communicate mainly through smells, and according to Jonathan, those smells volatilize even in the coldest weather. "It's not safe, that many VOCs," he said. "Another goddamn problem I have to solve."

We were not long in the field before Jonathan began refusing to leave the buggy. He began by sending me on sample expeditions while I was out surveying, each day requesting more, taking more of my time, keeping me from my survey work and slowing down our progress. We had a row on the topic, and he flat refused to exit anymore. I do not know what it was that he wished to avoid—I still do not—but he refused, and I am to small to force him, and I was unwilling to use a weapon to threaten him, and so his decision stuck.

My Qi found me when Jonathan was back in the buggy working in his lab, and I was in the field doing a soil structure survey. I caught the barest whiff, like blueberry wine, and turned around to see her poking her head out of a hollow. She turned her head left and right, catching me in each of her three large, flat eyes.

Then, after a long moment, she disappeared, leaving the smell of marigolds in her wake.

I had never seen one up close before, only from a distance. Everywhere we stopped seemed to have one patrolling its territory, but they never approached. I turned off the GPR and recorded a description before I lost the details, then went on with my work.

She came back. Often. Each time a little closer. Each time a little bolder, until I took to carrying a puff pistol with me. I did not know whether she considered me food or not. She certainly had the teeth and claws of a predator.

But she did not threaten me. She made near approaches, and wafted different odors my way at different times. And different smells seemed to be associated with differences in the texture around her face.

"Tell me something, Jonathan," I asked over dinner, "is it possible to communicate with smells?"

"Most animals do. Even we do, or we used to. Our noses don't work as well anymore, but we still signal stress and arousal and things like that."

"What about a real language?"

"Why do you ask?"

So I told him about my pet Qi, him listening all the while.

"Interesting." He chewed a mouthful of the galaxy's most boring rations, as if they were the stuff of revelation. "Take some samples tomorrow when he shows up. Make some notes. We could use this."

"Oh?"

"I don't have samples of local pheromones yet."

He did not elaborate. I did not ask him. Jonathan communicates molecular biology to the layperson as well as he dances.

The conversation died out. I crawled into my bunk and wondered how long I would be able to fit in the little shelf bunk before I swelled so big I had to sleep on the floor, or in the cab. She was big enough now that I could feel her twitching from time to time. If I had been alone, I would have sung her to sleep, but Jonathan complained when I tried that, so I only did it in my mind.

The next day I began gathering pheromones, using some traps that Jonathan made up for me. The mad doctor seemed to lose all interest in his main project and started obsessively synthesizing new versions. He had me rigorously catalog the beast's behavior and appearance for every different odor.

"Try this," he said a few days later, handing me a folded card. "Use the spritzers like, I don't know, smoke signals or something. This is what I think they mean. I'd assume the creature..."

"Qi."

"What?"

"I discovered the species, I get to name them. They're called Qi."

"Okay, I'd assume the Qi is dangerous, and do nothing to attract or provoke it. Treat it like a tiger. You know, don't let it eat you, cause it's a long drive back for one person." And I swear, I thought I saw him smile, just a little.

The next morning, when I smelled blueberry wine, I read "curiosity" on the key card. I replied with a spritz of curiosity myself.

The Qi bayed. I turned to see her standing not ten meters away. When I met her eyes, she reared her head and started pacing back and forth in a line, as if a fence held her back. Perhaps she was waiting for permission? According to the card, "Vanillin 3" was supposed to mean "interest."

It sniffed the air, huffed, approached. Lemony musk reached for my nostrils. "Excitement."

I sprayed caution.

She wafted trust.

We went back and forth like that, a dance of odors that I

did not completely understand. But in a few moments, the creature was sitting next to me, swiping my legs tentatively with her tail, then dragging it across her nose, as if it were trying to make sure it understood me.

Close up, I could see its teeth—rows and rows of them, like a shark—lined up inside her hard bottom jaw. A hook on the underside of the jaw looked as if it might be adapted to use as an extra hand for climbing, or for striking killing blows with her chin. And its body rippled beneath the feathers and fur. Even ankle-deep in snow, she seemed perfectly warm, and so long as she kept swishing her fluffy, whip-like tail across me, I figured I was safe.

SHE BECAME MY REGULAR companion after that. When I worked outside, she worked alongside me. She did not exactly try to help, but she stuck close by and studied me, as if she had decided I was no threat, but did not know how else to consider me. I kept my pistol in my belt, just in case, but I never had to reach for it. Instead, I ran Jonathan's atomizers dry communicating with the creature.

"I think I will hate for to leave here tomorrow," I told him over dinner the last night of my survey, "I wonder if she will follow us."

"Don't bet on it. You're not near that cute."

I smiled despite his gruffness. I had never ranked Jonathan high up on the social skills ladder. In his eighty-four subjective years, he had never learned the utility of courtesy or personability, and traveling with him, I found it remarkably easy to stir his anger to a boil—much more than he had been back at camp. More, for certain, than he should have, given the mission gods and their protocols, but, nevertheless, something about the expedition had pushed him to the edge. But for those few days, he seemed to decide we were fellow soldiers.

That night, in my bunk, I spoke in my head to the little one inside me. I told her of the things I was learning about this place, the strangeness and the sameness together that made up a recipe of wonder. A world where smells are a kind of language, and you can communicate with the sub-sentient wildlife using perfume bottles.

When we left the next morning, the Qi followed us for the next thirty klicks, until we passed the far borders of her territory.

Somewhere in my time with the Qi, my soul arrived at the conviction that this world had to be shared, and had to be protected. As she disappeared behind the ridge in the hindview, I patted my belly and whispered "I'll introduce you when you're old enough."

Things change when you get pregnant. They change more when you decide to keep it. This was her world now, as far as I was concerned. I was going to make sure she could live in it.

Expedition: Filbert
Mission Day 450
Mission Historian Personal Perspective
Year 2253 of the Common Era

THE REAL STORMS STARTED IN our seventh week out. We were deep in a hidden valley by a bend in the river when we got the text flash from base on the short-wave mast.

Emergency. Cyclone approaching. Category Three. 200kph winds from southwest. Expect flash flooding. Find shelter on high ground and wait out.

"Flash floods?" I said, "In the middle of winter?"

"I'm not a climatologist, don't look at me."

I did not look at him, but then I did not look at him very

often anymore. The fellow-feeling we had built through my experiments communicating with the Qi on our journey had all but evaporated in the weeks since. Perhaps it was that he believed it was my fault we were out here on this ridiculous trip—even though it was his idea, and the opprobrium he suffered at the hands of our colleagues was also the result of him opening his big mouth in a meeting, knowing it would make him unpopular—or perhaps it was just because he did not approve of the noises I make in my sleep. Whatever it was, he had grown, in recent weeks, to loathe me more than life itself, and loathed it even more when he needed my help.

And he did need my help frequently. His experimental animals required tending, and he had succeeded in force-growing some rabbits that could subsist on local plant life, at least so far.

High ground is not an easy thing to find that deep in the canyon. The best we could do was scout—quickly and on foot—for an upstream shelf that might keep us far enough out of the wind and high enough out of the water to survive the night.

THE RIVER DID, IN FACT, rise. A sleet slurry, thick with ice, moving like a cryonic ooze within a meter or two of our little cliff. Fish-like creatures, no larger than a child's hand, teemed in the water—on gentle days I would watch them through the windows, like a billion small salmon running to the sea.

The winds bashed into the broad side of our mobile laboratory like a legion of angry Qi. We both of us were motion-sick for the first two days. Four days later, the buggy was still swaying like a ship on the high seas, but by then we had our sea legs, so to speak.

With no way to do my own work, I played the part of

Jonathan's reluctant laboratory assistant. From time to time he attempted to explain to me what he was doing, but I do not have the background to reiterate even the parts I understood. At least, not in any depth. The best I could tell was that he was working on some kind of digestive enzyme that could break down the offensive molecules so that humans could digest them. A new secretory gland paired with the salivary glands, or with the stomach lining—he was attempting both, in hopes that at least one would work. If he could pull it off, it would mean we could modify ourselves *in situ* without any of those pesky ethical problems.

Hope, as my mother would say, is a thin reed, easily snapped in the wind.

Five weeks later, still stranded in our little lab, we ran to the last of our food. The mission's provisions were designed to be supplemented by protein and plants grown in a greenhouse on the roof, but the sunlight had been so wan, the periodic eclipses so deep, and the clouds so constant that nothing much grew up there. About all we had for fresh were the mushrooms in the underfloor bed.

The power situation was not much better. The buggy was meant to run on solar during the day and bioreactives at night, a regular alternating cycle that the engineers back at base had optimized for the long days and nights on Filbert. The little creatures in the bioreactive compartments needed their downtime to allow the support organisms to process their waste into a form that would not poison the colony—and to allow the thin-film capacitors to charge up and supply them with "the seed energy that keeps their whole self-contained ecosystem functioning within normal parameters" as Christiana would say.

JONATHAN'S MOOD HAD GROWN dour, even surly, and he no longer suffered my assistance in the laboratory. He worked himself, day and night, sleeping in odd increments on something he called a "Fuller Cycle." When I asked what that meant, he grumbled about how only an idiot didn't know about polyphasic sleep and I should just go drown in the river.

So I spent long hours confined to my bunk, or pacing back and forth in the little cab, trying to figure out ways to stay alive when the crisis came. I knew it would come. Anyone who could not see that, as far as I was concerned, did not deserve to stay alive.

Though I did not want to do it, we really only had one option.

"Field team to base, field team to base, come back. Come back."

The radio returned static.

"Field team to base, field team to base, this is Chan Xiyi at..." I read the coordinates from our satellite feed. "We are stranded on a high shelf, losing power, low on food. We need the cropper down for immediate evac. Over."

Nothing.

I kept at it for nearly an hour, and only stopped because Jonathan started screaming for me to shut up and let him work in peace. They had chosen him for his ability to focus on work under pressure, now his inability to task-switch meant that I was the only hope for all three of us.

"What in the blue devil would you have me to do? Just sit out here and die?"

"How about trying to shut the FUCK up and letting me work?"

"How about..." I stopped. We had been around this track many, many times in the last weeks. It never worked. Jonathan was incapable of subtext. Sarcasm, invective, anything indirect blew past him like the wind past our buggy. "Jonathan, if I do not find a way to get us out of here, your work will never find an audience. It will all be for nothing. We will die here, and soon. Do you understand?"

He claimed he did.

"I need some fresh air." I shrugged into a parka, tied on my snow pants and shoes. Even with those, I'd only survive a few minutes outside. But those few minutes perhaps would give me some kind of solution.

There is a level of cold that reaches down your throat and sinks its claws into your soul, and takes pieces of it away. A phantom, hungry and remorseless.

The baby was hungry too. I could feel her twisting and grasping. It could feel my anxiety, and dread.

I did not get much farther than the doorstep of our little shelter. In the light reflected from one of the other moons of the gas giant, I took in the drifting snow, piled up far enough now that we would need a spring thaw just to move out of here. The sleet river still flowed within a meter or two of the bank, only now it teemed with what looked like eels, writhing in frenzy over and around one another, like snakes in a frying pan.

In another world, on another planet, where the chemistry was just a little different, I could make a spear, and bring it inside, and cook it, and eat.

When food runs thin and power runs cold, you begin to think of impossible things. Dreams. Plans. Dark and unthinkable things. They made me shudder more than the cold.

I went back inside before I froze. At least in there I would not have to look at animals that I could not eat.

"They *what?*" Jonathan thundered when I told him. Proper yelling. Rageful, even. The kind of sound that makes a person look around to find a hole to crawl into, only there were no holes in our little buggy. I had not quite started waddling yet, but I could barely fit into my bunk slot anymore.

"They grew. Two meters each. More, maybe, some of them."

"So go get one."

"And why? For what good would it do?"

He huffed, rolled his eyes. "Protein source, for the experiment. You really don't have any brains at all, do you?"

I bit my tongue. Never in my life have I had a relationship of any kind that made me afraid of what to say next, every time I spoke. Anything I said would make things worse. Even to give in.

"See?" He waved both his arms in front of my face. "Not a thing. Can't even see why they shipped your sorry twat up here."

 I finally mumbled "It does not matter."

"What did you say?"

"I said it matters for crap because when the power runs out we will all three of us be dead anyway in a few days."

"Three."

"Yes, three."

"So you *are* pregnant."

I was not as surprised as you might expect. Jonathan's observational powers ended at his petri dishes. "Do you want me to go get one of those eels or not?"

He sneered at me, which I took for a yes.

Initialization

Swarming out, refugees from a dying universe.
Adrift upon endless eddies, a lifeline, not an expedition.
The colonists for a distant world, fertile with possibilities.
A last, undreamt-of hope
Landing, at last, and barely, on alien soil.

Chapter 10

Obligations

IN THE FOUNDATION'S LIBRARY, on this final night before upload, the candlelight at the lone table cast everything in the glow of future memory. Daimler's knife nicked the caramelized crust of the six ounce camel tenderloin. The brown split like the skin of a peach, pushing the moist muscle beneath up to protrude slightly over the surface.

"Perfect," Daimler said. "Eat up. It's the last fresh meal you'll get in a good long while. Pay attention to how the tamarind garum matches the loin to the asparagus and the mango."

Xiyi turned her attention to her own, matching meal. Four months ago she'd never have touched camel, being a woman of limited palate and particular tastes, but part of indoctrination meant opening up her tastes, in all ways, so that she would be able to adapt to whatever the new planet threw at her. Daimler had been an excellent guide, helping her learn to write in the ways that would be most useful to the mission, coaching her all through on techniques to deal with the isolation she'd feel as the team's lone observer, helping her master the difference between the formal reports and the personal observations, and all of it somehow while immersed in the wonder she'd always had where words were concerned.

The meat melted on her tongue, like something between venison and horse, salty and gamey, the sauce wrapping around her tongue and marrying it to the exotic flesh before her throat closed around it.

Xiyi found her way past her inchoate noises of pleasure to say "Exquisite. Lovely. Thank you."

"You noticed the sauce?"

"It's perfect. It makes everything work."

"Enjoy. And think on it. Starting tomorrow, you are the sauce. Your ability to read *and* feel *and* express emotions puts you in the position of translator, should it become necessary. If we're right about how this should work, if our experiments in Antarctica are telling the truth, you'll become the glue that holds it all together. And as mission chronicler, you're the one we depend on for an accurate picture of the human element."

"Yes, yes, we have talked about this before." Xiyi tried a bite with a bit of mango and asparagus on the fork at the same time, with a little wasabi from the garnish. Her sinuses opened up and the flavor bloomed in a way it hadn't the first time around. If she got lucky, he'd let her relax instead of going through the pop quiz routine that Christiana had warned her about earlier today before she went into terminal processing.

"Yes, we have, and it's important that you have it burned into your synapses."

"That is an intrinsic part of reassembly process, is it not?"

"You know what I mean."

"Very well." Xiyi sighed, giving up on her fantasy of her last meal being purely a sensualist's affair.

"So, let's assume that something goes drastically wrong. A write-error in someone's synapses, or an unforeseen circumstance causing unresolvable friction. How do you spot it? What are the danger signs?"

"Again?"

"If you don't know this, you won't be able to accurately record what's going on. Now, tell me again."

"The stables withdraw. Become less sociable than they are naturally inclined."

"Start at the top. What are the danger signs with command?"

"The healthy non-narcissistic psychopath will do what he feels has to be done. Trouble signs include a withdrawal from normal command style, indulging in status displays, subtle shows of dominance outside his normal behavior patterns, pronounced deception and manipulation for strategic reasons instead of just screwing with people for fun. In extremis, for example, when plotting an execution or a permanent change, he will have an intellectual justification that can be checked by those to whom he is accountable, and he will tailor the presentation to the tastes of the audience. When pressed and not feeling under threat if he is honest, he will give direct account of his own internal reasoning, and may brag about it."

"Correct. And the stables?"

"Stables have normal emotional responses, but have a different relationship with their emotions than I do. They feel things very strongly, and resent being perceived as overemotional. In extremis, they will rationalize. When feeling vulnerable, they will personalize slights and insults. When contemplating violence, they will aggressively demean and depersonalize the object of their malice. Their internal justifications for aggression are based on righteousness rather than on expediency, and they are more prone to create justifications for punishment than to bow to the exigencies of fate." She realized she was reciting from the book, almost verbatim.

"And as chronicler? When you begin to see these unhealthy patterns emerging?"

"To document. Both by direct observation and by analysis—and when possible, to obtain direct testimony from the parties involved and document that as well."

"And how will you secure that testimony?"

"I am bound by an oath of confidentiality, no different than a doctor or a lawyer. I may only break it under conditions of imminent violence, and only to the department head or command officer who is, in my judgment, best equipped to deal with the situation."

"Good."

He spoke through the rest of dinner, drilling her on the differences between her regular reports and her daily journals, the forms for formal incident write-ups, the mission priorities, the particular points of interest the Foundation had in the interaction within her particular team, and the rest of her endless list of responsibilities, caveats, goals, and limitations.

"Now that that's settled," he said with a clap of his hand, "I believe it's time for the dessert."

The dinner service bot obliged with chocolate soufflé and champagne. He held his flute up to her and said, "You've done well, Xiyi. I expect great things. You will make this world as proud as you have already made me."

She blushed, and drank, and inside, where she shook from apprehension, she took a little comfort in the fact that she was as prepared as anybody could be for the last step into the unknown.

Alarm

Darkness swallowed the heights, the depths, the air itself.
The eyes and ears, zipping round, fell endlessly in a sky grown quiet.
The beacons failed. Grew silent. Winked out.
Nothing reached them. An exigency long expected, longer dreaded.
But they could not execute their instructions until they finished their harvest in the tractless belts where the antimatter flowed, sparse as baby's hair, on the magnetic storms.
And the planet, cocooned in water-glass, grew quieter still.

Chapter 11

The Only Choice

Expedition: Filbert
Mission Day 455
Mission Historian Personal Perspective
Year 2253 of the Common Era

FIVE MORE DAYS. Still no word from base. We had four brown-outs, fifteen arguments, two episodes of near-freezing. I took to cycling the bioreactors out, running the buggy on half at a time, staying bundled up, going without light or computers most of the time, except for the radio and Jonathan's lab bench.

We managed, for a time, not to freeze. Food was a different matter.

"It's a proof-of-concept," Jonathan said, when he showed me his first successful batch, "This culture produces an enzyme that pre-digests the eel flesh, rendering it nutritionally accessible. Think of it like a kind of fish yogurt."

"And this is how you think we will survive here?"

Of course not. I was an idiot, too much of my brain siphoned off by my "little parasite" to think sensibly. This was just a proof-of-concept, and the next step was to figure out how to integrate this into an implantable organ or synthesize it for large-scale pre-processing of food that somehow stayed palatable. The applications were complicated, but there were many possibilities, and it was only my small-minded youthful idiocy that kept me from seeing what a brilliant advancement this was, assuming we could get back to base before we died. Now, if I would just shut up, he might grace me with a little bit of the pap for a taste test.

My mouth watered like spring thaw, and when he gave it to me I nearly shoveled the pasty eel into my mouth. It tasted like ox musk and vomit, and had the texture of wheat porridge, but it was protein. After a fashion. It took four tries to keep it down, and after that I decided I would rather starve.

The baby, though, had other ideas. I came back three more times that day.

"It won't work, you know," he said without looking up from his bench. "It's just protein. No micronutrients."

"Well, what do you suggest?"

He got that squirrelly look again. He did that any time the subject of food came up. If I pushed, he would just start yelling, and I did not have the patience. So I sighed and crawled into the nest I had made for myself on the floor, and wrapped my blankets around me.

Jonathan returned to his bench, and his tinkering. "You're gonna have to face it, you know," he said.

"Oh?" I pulled the blankets tighter around me. "What's that?"

"You're going to lose that parasite." He seemed to choke the word out, as if he were trying to convince himself. "It's probably already brain damaged. And it's the only thing we have to eat. Only question is whether we take it out now or we wait till you pass it and maybe it kills you."

"You...you..."

"You asked. Don't look at me like that. You think I like

it?" He pushed his microscope aside and rubbed his bluing fingers into his hollow, ashen-gray cheeks. "Doesn't matter. We'll freeze to death first anyway."

He swore. I barely noticed. I curled tighter into myself, as if my blankets could protect me and my baby from the world that seemed bent on ending us even as I tried to find a way to save it. But all I could hear was Jonathan's words, hammered into me over the last days. *Parasite. Parasite. Parasite.* As if it was not a near full-term baby.

I MUST HAVE FALLEN asleep then, from my hunger. I awoke some time later to the sound of labored breathing. I did not open my eyes, lest he see me, but after a moment I realized he was crying. Guilt over his determination to eat my baby? Hopelessness that we would not survive no matter what we did? I do not know. I suppose I never will.

He pulled himself together and started speaking to the computer. A standard log entry, audio summarizing his notes, everything beamed up to the sat network in real-time so that all our other stations could access it, if anyone out there was alive anymore.

After he finished, I heard his desk light go off. He stood, crossed the little room. I dared a crack in my eyelids in time to see him crawling into his bunk and curling up into a fetal position.

I suppose it must have been the hunger—hunger so bad you cease being hungry, and you begin to simply exist in a cloud of white noise, as if every thought exists only on the other side of a heavy mist. A cloud of dis-understanding that stood in my way kept me from comprehending my actions. But I understand now. And I will make it right.

The thing is, two lives are more important than one.

Especially if one of those lives has never had a chance to really live. And we could survive longer on him than he and I could on the baby. So as he slept, crying in his sleep about how low we had both sunk, I applied an anesthetic swab to his wrist and opened the vein with one of his laboratory scalpels.

I am no fool. I tied a bag over his wrist to catch the blood. The blood alone would sustain us for days.

He never knew he was anything but asleep. I dragged him outside and dressed his body—his carcass—as best I could manage. I knew that one must not pierce the organs, for fear of infection, and not break the spinal cord, for fear of prions. I saved the liver, and the kidneys, for the nutrition. I left the rest for the snow.

I do not remember much else. I did not wish to at the time. I had to work as if he were a kill from a hunt, and we were on a planet where we could actually eat what we caught. As if I was not butchering the body of someone I knew. Someone I cared about, even if I could not stand him. A friend, even.

Jonathan had been my last hope for humanity on Filbert, and for all his faults, he was an honest man.

—

I WENT NUMB AFTER that. I cooked bits of food in the microwave, and ate it without tasting it. I continued sending distress signals to base, and receiving nothing. I kept what I could of him in the refrigeration unit, and refreshed its cold with snow from outside to save on power. I dared not leave it out for the Qi, who smelled him soon after and came to scavenge his organs from the ground, then circled the buggy endlessly. Fighting. Retching. Baying. Waiting for the next free meal. Our meat, it seems, did not kill them, sick and mad as it seemed to drive them.

The night after, two of the bioreactors quit entirely. I gathered all the bedclothes from both slots, and the mattresses, and wrapped myself in my nest on the floor. I cooed at my baby, urging her to be strong, to soak up the good food, and not to quit on me, and that I was doing all of this for her. My world contracted to the limits of my blankets. I hibernated.

An eternity later—enough time that I had gone through an arm and two legs—the radio crackled.

"Base to Canyon Expedition."

I thought I was dreaming.

"Base to Canyon Expedition. Are you still there? We are prepping a rescue flight to your location. Are you still active? Can you still hear us? Come back."

The only way I would ever hear Dar's voice again is if I was dreaming. And yet here it was, bulldozing through my consciousness like fire through tissue paper.

He called again.

I stirred. I made my way to the radio. I wondered if there was anything left in the batteries to send with.

"Here. Here. Come get me. Please. Over."

"Are you still at the same location?"

"Yes. Ice-bound. Trapped. Please. Please come. Please. Please." I broke down. I kept speaking through my sobs, even though I did not know what it was I said. I had to get home. To where it was warm. To where I could eat something that didn't make me feel less human. To where I could give birth to my baby. To where I could make up for my actions.

THE SEMI-DIRIGIBLE CROPPER settled low over the buggy, and Dar abseiled down with Horace, one of Christiana's assistants. They shot some of the Qi, and scared some off.

"Xiyi, where is Jonathan?"

"He went home. He will meet us there." I did not know what else to say. I knew only my longing for warmth, for home. But I swore to myself I would bring him back. It would not be the same, he would not know me, but at least he would be alive. And he would help the rest of us survive.

Dar looked at me, unsure of what to make of my delirium, the nonsense in my words.

They took me up in a sling, to the heated cabin. The craft, loaded to capacity, hauled us across the sky, up the canyon, back to what used to be base. Along the way, they pried out of me the whole story, bit by bit, freeing the horror from the ice shield I had locked it behind.

The fields was covered in snow. Above the buildings, the mountain's glacier had grown, cantilevered over our little village like the threat of a father's angry fists. Half of the structures had fallen into disrepair, abandoned as if to a forgotten lover.

And, standing in the middle of it all, on a fully assembled gantry, a rocket topped with a little vehicle no larger than a rooftop water tank.

They had built the return ship.

"What...you have built the EER? Why?"

"A lot happened while you were gone, Xi. Not bad like what happened to you, but bad enough."

"But...but...we can't just *leave*. This is home. After all we've..."

"Sunk cost fallacy. If we stay we *will* all die before the winter ends. It took us two weeks to dig ourselves out from the last big storm. We lost our farm, half the hydroponics garden, two digger robots, and six good people. And yours is the only remote we managed to rescue. All that, Xi, from one series of storms. Nineteen dead in all, Xi. Nineteen. What happens with the next one?"

"But, but…"

"Shh." He kissed me. It felt like pressing a briefcase to my lips. Lifeless, unconnected, cold. As if my time in that buggy had removed from me any ability to touch another human being. "It's either this, or we're dead. Simple as that. We were getting ready for dust-off when we found your distress call in the satellite's archive."

"But we have power. Nuclear batteries here, not solar. We can survive. And Jonathan…Jonathan solved the protein problem. He got this enzyme, all in his logs. He cracked it. Another year of work and we can integrate somehow. Maybe with an augment. Great fuckings, Dar, we cannot just up and *leave* like this."

"I'm sorry. The decision is made. Once you're recouped enough for a stable upload, we'll flash-back you and process you."

"That…that…my baby…"

"Have to terminate. You can't upload an infant. You can't guarantee a stable upload until about ten years, you know that…"

"Dar, be…"

"Absolutely out of the question. Shh. Stop. No more questions."

I had nothing more to say anyway, so I did not.

I now realize, as I close out this chronicle and read it through entire, that all the time I was out in the field, a plan had been growing on my mind. An unthinkable plan, and yet it haunted my thoughts like the ghost of the woman I used to be. I never really believed it would work, or that I could do it.

For now, I just pressed my face to that window and watched as our little world rose up to meet us, and reflected on how much a person can change in such a short time.

Quickening

A campsite.
A village.
A town.
A city, sprouting into nationhood.
Stretching out its fingers into the void.
Clamping down upon the liquid universe.
And echoing, declaring, the soundless declaration: I.

Chapter 12

Upload

ONE WHITE SINGLETON WITH blue ribbon trim on one white table beneath the bright daylight-balanced bulbs of the upload clinic's restroom.

Xiyi's fingers found the edges. It unfolded, spreading the clinical scents of pine and lemons and iodine. She looked to her right, sizing herself up in the vanity mirror. Her chai skin looked sallow and jaundiced in the blue light, her squarish hips had gotten dumpy due to too much desk work, her breasts were falling, ever so slightly, to the south. It occurred to her that, as attached as she was to her body, she would not mourn its passing. On the other side, she'd get a body with fifteen more years on its clock, with none of those early-morning aches, the embarrassing scars on her knees, with the ability to stay up all night again without paying for it in a morning.

She draped the smock over her arms and pinched her thigh, the loose skin on her knees, ran her fingers over all the imperfections on her face and neck. The acne scars, and the broken nose from where she'd gotten into that fight with her brother over the rights to the clubhouse when she was twelve, and her parents had refused to let her get it fixed in order to "teach her a lesson." All the markers of bad decisions, good adventures, and her fundamental clumsiness. Not long now, and she'd be well rid of them.

As soon as she stopped stalling.

She stuck her arms through the holes in the smock. The ribbons she passed around her body and tied double in front of her, like a rear-entry kimono. With one more look at herself in the mirror, this time dressed like an institutional prisoner, she waved goodbye to her reflection.

The doors parted before her, giving her access to a short hall. At the end of the hall, another set of doors on swing hinges allowed her access to a large, tile-clad room. On one side, a glass-walled office containing the headers and control overrides for the treatment equipment. On the other, a standard surgical bed, fully outfitted with IV hookups for anesthesia and cryo, coupled to a neural scanner for upload, and some minor support equipment and furniture for the technicians—nothing that everyone who'd ever been in for surgery hadn't seen before. But this time, there was a second table, set off to the side, in front of a v-shaped fabric-fronted baffles.

Xiyi gave the technicians behind the glass a nervous wave, and made her way to the table by the baffles. Upon it, resting on a black velvet pillow as if it were a priceless jewel, a stainless steel long-barrel Buntline-style .44 magnum revolver—the kind that used chemical propellant in cartridges, rather than air pressure, to throw its slug. Next to it, a single long—impossibly long—cartridge lay sleeping on a pillow.

She approached and stretched her fingers toward it in almost religious reverence. She'd read about their mythic power since she was a child, but she had never been in the presence of one. Weapons in her world, even projectile weapons, worked largely on air pressure or induction.

Cool to the touch, but not cool like the dead. The different textures sent small electric shocks of excitement straight to the pit of her stomach. She could feel her chest tremble when she drew breath.

She felt as if she should say something cavalier, like people did in books, but she found herself unable to remember anything she would want to remember saying.

The stillness of the ventilation fans shattered with the whoosh of a motorized door made her jump. She turned to see the uploader, complete with labcoat and tablet, walking toward her as if she were the next vehicle in for service.

"People with their fetishes," he muttered, then looked up at Xiyi as if she were an afterthought. "You sure about this?"

"Which part?"

"All of it."

Her stomach did a little backflip. "Yes. Yes, I think so."

"Well, then. Stand with your back against the V, there. It says here, and I just need to verify, you see. Liability, see, so I need to verify what it says here, that you want to be shot before upload so you will retain the memory, is that right?"

Xiyi managed to make her head nod. She didn't dare respond out loud, in case they suddenly decided she was crazy and ejected her from the mission.

"Well, it's your skin. You realize you're going to have to do this yourself, right?"

"Mmm hmm."

"Okay. So, here's how it works." He took Xiyi by the shoulders and guided her directionless body over to the baffles, then left her there to stare at him while he reached under the table and deployed an articulated stand with a mount on the end of it. "The weapon goes here, secure it with these pins here and here. Make sure you secure the trigger loop. Once it's loaded and aimed, you yank the cord, and it sends the bullet straight through your body and into the bullet trap."

"Through?"

"Unless it gets caught on a bone, yeah. Even then it could break through. You wanted powerful, that's what you got. Now, you do the honors."

Xiyi took a moment to unfreeze. When she did, she found her hands trembling and fumbling, like a virgin in bed after too much beer, and struggling to undo a corset and buttons. The uploader tried to help her, but she batted him away. She knew how it worked, she'd just never thought she'd get her hands on one for real.

The cartridge slid into the cylinder. The cylinder clicked into place. She mounted the weapon on the arm, secured the clamps.

"Be sure to switch on the sight."

A laser, clamped to an under-sling on the impossibly long barrel. She pressed the button, and a green dot appeared on the baffles.

"Don't pull it until we give you the okay. We need to make sure you're not going to hit anything that will kill you too quickly."

Her feet started itching. Her hair felt like it was sweating. Cold bathed her from the base of her skull down to her anus. *Kills me too quickly. It really will kill me. I really will die.*

On leaden feet, she clomped in front of the sight. The uploader grabbed her upper arm, shuffled her slightly to the right. "There. This should go through-and-through your obliques, minimal organ damage. Should give us plenty of time. Now, we took your backup yesterday, so if anything happens, we will just use that upload for the restore at the far end, but if you survive this, it's this iteration that will go through. You understand, you will retain this memory, yes?"

"Yes."

"Press your thumbs here please."

Xiyi laid her thumbs on the proffered screen, pressed them down. The camera took her picture, recorded her authorization.

"Very well. Here's the cord. I'm going to cock the weapon for you, to ensure minimal disruption on the pull."

"Thank you."

The cylinder rotated, the hammer double-clacked. "Please wait until I'm behind the glass before you fire."

The uploader withdrew. Xiyi's eyes closed, as if on their own.

The cord swam in Xiyi's palms, slick as an eel. Her heart thrummed like an air compressor. Years seemed to pass between each breath.

Her life was almost over. No matter what else happened. Whether she uploaded, or whether something went wrong, she was one of the dead. Suddenly, that mattered in a way it hadn't before.

Xiyi opened her eyes, stared at the barrel, and ground her teeth together as if she were making bone powder. She did not want to die. She wanted to live.

But how could she live if she passed up a chance to see the other side of the galaxy? After this, what would ever convince her that she had the integrity, and the courage, to deserve her share of oxygen?

What was life, after all, if a woman stayed forever in her cradle, treating herself as a fragile thing?

Xiyi took one last breath.

She yanked.

The bullet tore through her abdomen, her blood spilled down her legs. Waves of burning, ripping numbness shook her. Euphoria boxed her in, trapped her with the pain inside her own skull. She felt hands on her, moving her, laying her out, staunching her bleeding. Hooking her up.

The machine scrutinized the map of her every sensation, every memory, every connection. A brilliant city in the darkness. The patterns changed as the shock settled in. Then, the drugs pulled her down the deep slope to the blackness. The lights went out, one by one, until the last axon sent its last impulse along the last neuron, across the last synapse, to the last dendrite, and the city went dark.

Chan Xiyi Aya breathed her last breath of her home planet.

And died.

Redemption

Pushing.
Ripping.
Holding.
Tearing.
Crowning.
Alone. But only just.
Screaming.
Crying.
Mewling.
Sighing.
Seeking.
Finding.
The last reason.
And also the first.

Chapter 13

In Service of the Future

Expedition: Filbert
Mission Day 623
Mission Historian Personal Perspective
Year 2254 of the Common Era

THIS IS MY FINAL ENTRY.

They say that when life closes a door it opens a window.

They know nothing.

When life locks you in a cell, you find a way out, or you go mad. It does not provide you with anything. You are always on your own, just as you have been ever since you fought your way out of your mother's body.

For the next four days I was on my own in that infirmary. Just me, alone with my convalescence. Dar had ordered the system to nurse me back to half-health so that I could survive the abortion, and give good quality upload, and go home with the rest of them.

I could hear the rest processing through in the next room. Two or three per day, the ones that were least needed to finish the fold-up of the base. Upload scan. Euthanization. Bodies shuttled into the fermentation chute to be processed for fertilizer. We would leave the buildings, properly winterized and locked down, in case the Foundation decided to send another expedition.

On the fourth day, Dar visited. He told me I was good enough to venture out for a couple hours. He needed to bring me up to date for my chronicle. Fill me in on what happened while I was gone. He would brief me, then we would return for the procedure, and I would recuperate, and then we would both stick around to supervise the last uploads, before going ourselves.

He told me the storm had hit them here harder than it had hit us down the canyon, at least to start. They'd moved the bulk of the colony into the main building and redirected most of the base's power to melting and diverting the ice and snow so it didn't bury them in drifts. With everyone, and all the robots, working round the clock, it took them days to realize they'd lost the radio mast in the storm's first assault.

By the time they got everything up and running, and recycled their dead, they'd lost six weeks. They found my distress calls. They found death calls from two of the other expeditions. They sent a retrieval ship for a third. It did not return.

Filbert was a death planet. Brutal biology, brutal geology, brutal winters. It had chewed us up and spit us out.

"Planet 1, humanity 0. We're done." Dar said. "What really happened out there?"

I did not really want to talk about it, but he was mission commander. I told him as little as I thought I could get away with. He didn't press.

"I can't imagine what it was like for you out there."

"What about Jonathan?"

He shook his head. "Nothing we can do."

"But his backup..."

"You remember indoctrination. You're the one that fretted

over what it would do to your soul. Do you really want to make a copy of him, have him lose everything since his first upload, re-orient him, tell him what happened and why he can't remember?"

He could read me, better than anyone. I did not know exactly what he might see, but it terrified me, so I did not dare look him in the face. "Won't they for to restore him back home?"

He scowled. "It's against the law."

"Yeah, I guess so."

He took my hand. "I'm just glad you made it back in one piece. And we got his notes. Hey," he crooked his finger under my chin, pulled my eyes from the snowy ground, "don't do that. The next team they send, when they send it, will be able to do something with this place. The data we've put together will let them come up with a plan that can work even here. If people can live on Europa...well, we'll be here eventually."

"Just not today?"

"Just not today. But I'm glad it was you that came back." He kissed me. "I missed you. A lot, really. Place is colder without you."

I soft-punched his arm. "Pillock. They call it 'winter'."

"That too." He looked at the sky. "Time to get inside. Let's get you taken care of."

We shuffled through the fallow furrows to the infirmary. He waved me in before him with a gallant gesture, and I disappeared behind a dressing screen while he saw to selecting the procedure from the robot.

"How far along are you?"

"Eight months. Maybe a little more." I looked around for anything I could use. Anything I was sure about.

"Okay." In the silence, while he navigated the machine, I

found a good solid pen. Once I had it, I slipped out of my clothes and pulled a smock. "We'll have it do a D&E."

"I want full anesthesia. I do not want to have any memory."

"You got it."

I adjusted my smock, covered the pen in my crossed arms, and remembered the frenetic music they played in the Fear Club on Phobos Station that time I wound up there. I remembered the muscle and sweat. I remembered the beat. And the shrieking vocalists and the thickness of life in that crowded little room.

The fast beat set in my brain.

A metronome.

A guide.

I emerged from behind the screen and approached the chair.

"God you look amazing."

"Helpless sickos are your thing?"

"Just you. I hope when we get home...?"

"Come here." I reached for him with both hands. He stepped into my arms, and I kissed him. We swayed to the beat in my head. I ran my hands across his back, down his arms. I held on as long as I dared.

When my left hand reached his shoulder, I gripped the pen tight, and plunged it into his neck, then pulled out, then plunged. On the beat. Over and over. Forty, fifty times.

His life, like crushed tomatoes, splashed all over the room.

He didn't cry out. He just wheezed, clutching his throat, staring in uncomprehending surprise.

I held him as he fell, and I wept over him as his breath whistled wetly through the holes in his windpipe. "Sorry I am so sorry Dar I just, I just, my baby, I could not, not our baby.

Not here. I just..."

I could not bring myself to say what was in my heart, and I did not know what else to say. But the last of his blood washed over my thighs, and his skin went cold, and it did not matter anyway.

With Dar gone, it left four in the compound, including me. I held my ground until dinner, then smuggled a measure of cytoklazine into the evening meal, and went without myself.

I fed the bodies into the recycling plant, where they would be broken down to fertilizer, and fuel, and amino acids to keep us alive.

—

THE FLOODS BROKE WHEN the spring came. The world went from stick-brown to purple. I saw Qi in the forest before it thickened up, before their feathers made them disappear into the underbrush. We saw flying creatures—resembling enormous, fuzzy bats—for the first time since our arrival.

The base, too, found its spring. I waited until my little Tzu—a boy, it seems, and not a girl at all—was old enough to crawl on his own, working as I could, before I set the machinery to work on bootstrapping.

Restored from backups, every one. I owed them that much. The growth cycle and capacity meant I had to do them in batches. I brought the biochemists back first. Jonathan first. I owed it to him. He oversaw the rest.

"The climate on this world," I told them when we all assembled, "Ruined this expedition once, before we all finished waking up. Those of you who were waking, died in the first weeks. I survived only by the kindness of Dr. Galbraith, who saw to it that my baby and I would survive. He put us in stasis in the infirmary, so that we could wait out the winter, and spent the last of his life leaving us the legacy to survive. He backed himself up when he could not work anymore, but that module we lost in the storms. Dr. Galbraith, you have been restored from your original backup—I am confident that this would not disturb you, in these rare circumstances."

"Not at all. Thank you, Xi."

"You are welcome." I fought past the catch in my throat. I cleared it, and raised my voice, so they would not notice. "The orbit of this planet and its biochemistry present significant challenges. I have been entrusted with the information necessary for us to push forward and establish our colony before we are all frozen by the next ice age."

They believed me. I had no reason, after all, to lie. I am the normal one. The glue. The interface and the chronicler. History is my responsibility. Whatever I say happened, happened.

I have not told them who little Tzu's father is. Why should I? It has nothing to do with any of them. His father—his real father—is dead. My words killed him. My promises to my son.

We are on track to winterize the colony, and Tzu is starting to walk. He will grow up knowing Filbert as his home, with its nebulae and gas giants in the sky, and its purple vegetation, and the perilous Qi who he can talk to once I teach him.

And I will teach him.

At night, some times, I leave him in bed and walk outside, and watch the heavens whirl above us. I can see the satellites passing over us like guardian angels. I look at them and I miss my friends. The real ones. I am surrounded now by shadows. Fleshy ghosts. I still do not know if they are real.

But for Tzu, they are real. And at least I will see him grow up, and live in this place, and face horizons I cannot yet imagine.

Upon transmission of this chronicle, I shall delete all local copies. My memories, if the universe permits, will fade as well. They too, will be only ghosts, and then nothing.

I, Chan Xiyi Aya, write this. In service of the future.

THE END

EXTRAS

About the Author

While Star Wars and Star Trek seeded J. Daniel Sawyer's passion for the unknown, his childhood in academia gave him a deep love of history and an obsession with how the future emerges from the past. This obsession led him through adventures in the film industry, the music industry, venture capital firms in the startup culture of Silicon Valley, and a career creating novels and audiobooks exploring the worlds that assemble themselves in his head. His travels with bohemians, burners, historians, theologians, and inventors led him eventually to a rural exile where he uses the quiet to write, walk on the beach, and manage a pair of production companies that bring innovative stories to the ears of audiences across the world.

Author's Note

THE FUTURE IS A STRANGE PLACE, and for a science fiction writer, it's a moving target. Already, a number of assumptions that underlie my series The Antithesis Progression are starting to look a little obsolete. I only mention that here, because for those of you who are interested in Meta-continuity, I wanted to confirm what you already suspect: that this story does, indeed, take place in the Antithesis universe, and is part of the future of those characters.

Which doesn't have a lot else to do with this book. The story of The Resurrection Junket is a bit orthogonal to all that.

Some stories come from your soul. Some emerge from the struggle to stay disciplined in your work. Some write themselves from the right jumping off point. Some are things you plot for years, and craft. Some are impulses of delight.

There is another kind, perhaps the rarest kind—at least for me—which burst in upon you in one moment where something about the world locks, teeth-and-sprocket, with something inside you.

The Resurrection Junket was one of these rarest sorts. It found me at exactly the right moment--the best moment a story like this can find you: on a Saturday morning when your plans have just been completely ruined.

Now, a lot of things can happen on a Saturday, particularly when your Saturday begins with the sound of a large clambering lorry getting stuck in your cul-de-sac. It had been a particularly late Friday night, the night before, and even with earplugs there was no way I was getting back to sleep with that unholy racket pounding on my windows--not with a three-digit temperature in the making and no air conditioning.

These are the kinds of things you learn the hard way trying to make your living as a writer in one of the most expensive areas on the planet.

At the time, Saturday mornings were also one of my prime audiobook recording times, but a moment of connecting the concepts of "ambient noise" and "recording session" convinced me that even an attempt would be a fool's errand.

A peek out the front door also confirmed my most surly suspicions: I could forget about going out anywhere that might have air conditioning, or indeed people more civilized than I am. I was trapped by the wedged tractor-trailer, which was itself blocked in by a labyrinthine construction zone and a half-assed detour, preventing it from getting to the neighborhood market just down the road.

It is times like this when the Internet's more trivial uses (such as streaming video) reveal themselves to be the hidden godsends that they are. I spent the morning padding out my biotech education by catching up on talks from Craig Venter (the father of synthetic biology) and Juan Enriquez (his business partner and author of As The Future Catches You, a book about anticipatory investing and policymaking).

This little odyssey through YouTube-land eventually led me to a fascinating little tête à tête between Ray Kurzweil and Juan Enriquez sponsored by the folks at TED.

Now, how to describe Kurzweil...

If you've ever seen or used a Kurzweil synthesizer, you've heard Ray's name. A musical prodigy and inventor who was one of the pioneers in electronic music, he's one of the few from that era who managed to turn his passion into a successful business (or, in his case, a series of them). A great example of a driven autodidact and integrative thinker, if a little...well, nutty.

Lately he's gotten a lot more famous for being a kook on the optimistic fringe. His optimism is born from his skill for projecting technological development curves and starting products and companies designed to take advantage of where the market is likely to be, and he's pretty damn good at this, but when he applies this method toward predicting the progress of human civilization the results range from interesting to exciting to kinda scary to just plain bugnutty.

Enriquez, by contrast, is not a futurist—he's an investor and a sometimes-diplomat, and his work as a public intellectual and educator is concerned chiefly with resilience and awareness. His maxim for understanding how life and technology intersect, "All life is code," is one of the quotes that open The Resurrection Junket.

To Enriquez's mind, understanding where things are, technologically speaking at any given moment, is essential to surviving and thriving under the conditions they will generate on the ground in a few years time. That technological state of play is miles away from where most people think it is--miles ahead, always. He believes that a good understanding of the current wavefront of research in a given field (rather than the current position of that field in the marketplace) will give his audience (investors, venture capitalists, entrepreneurs, and sometimes lawmakers) the equivalent of headlights on a dark road.

In other words, Kurzweil is a madcap futurist, and Enriquez is a hard-nosed present-based pragmatist. Their interests are complimentary, but their approaches diverge significantly.

Frankly, I hadn't expected I would ever get to see the two of them trade ideas in this kind of open forum. The hour-long discussion is well worth a watch, even though it is now (at only a year old) starting to show its age in the details.

I was half-watching, half-listening to this conversation while cleaning my living room when something grabbed me and made me run it back. After forty minutes of talking about recent advances in neurohacking (such as the ability to read, write, and manipulate memories using lasers and photochemicals, which is now a proven technology still in its infancy, thanks to some clever folks at MIT), the quinary data density of DNA and its potential as a self-repairing data storage medium, the current research in regenerative medicine, the ability to de-extinct animals by using artificial life techniques, the reality of 3D printing, etc. the moderator asked a question about how these technologies might intersect.

Juan Enriquez answered with a laundry list of all the technologies above, and then said that: "If you could do all that, there isn't any reason you couldn't have travel over very long distances using cells as opposed to bodies."

This, from the mouth of the man whose maxim is "All life is code."

There was a quiet moment from the audience, and then a quiet gasp as everyone digested the implications of what he was talking about.

I ran that bit back a few times, watching it over and over, because I could feel the teeth of the universe locking with the sprockets of my mind. An hour later, I had the first thousand words of a new novel called The Resurrection Junket down on the page. You hold the result in your hand.

Either, or both, Enriquez and Kurzweil may be wrong about some of the the implications they see about the trajectory of the future, but at bottom they are both right about something: What is going on, right now, technologically is upending and re-framing questions that used to be purely speculative and philosophical. The nature of life, the nature of consciousness, the existence (or not) of the soul, the nature of the universe, the very definition of what it means to be human—all of these things are now up in the air due to hard facts on the ground, rather than just the dictates of logic.

The future is a strange place—the present is even stranger. But there has never been a better, safer, more interesting time to be alive, and tomorrow looks even moreso.

Acknowledgements

WHILE WITH THIS ONE, THE story came easily, how to tell it proved an interesting challenge. Nathan Lowell and Kitty Nic'Iaian are the chief reasons this book saw the light of day. Their invaluable feedback and quality-control eyes allowed me to find the way through the unusual structure of The Resurrection Junket.

Chris Lester, Adam McCullough, Lucie LeBlanc and Sue Taliaferro gave me first eyes and an invaluable clarity check. Their varying levels of expertise helped me keep the science accurate and intelligible while keeping the story front-and-center in front of the technology.

Special thanks to Dawn Phynix for her help voice-checking Xiyi's narration and speaking voice against the grammatical constructions of contemporary (and likely-to-evolve) Panglish, which is Xiyi's first language.

Finally, and this may be odd to put in an acknowledgments section, I can't thank enough my friends in the Valley, who keep me in touch with the craziness that passes for everyday life in the offices and laboratories the future passes through. The Sand Hill and Stanford tech center firms are not the center of the world anymore, but they do have their finger on the pulse. May they continue to live in interesting times.

If you enjoyed *The Resurrection Junket*,
you might also enjoy the following sample of

J. Daniel Sawyer's

Predestination
(and Other Games of Chance)
Book I of *The Antithesis Progression*

Grissom Spaceport, Luna City
9 October, 2129
1420 Hours GMT

THURSTON APPLEBEE SHAW SHIFTED HIS gaze down from the lightpipe panels. His attempt to abate his irritation with a disciplined count to ten was about as successful as his boyhood attempts to teach voles to fetch.

Then again, he thought as his eyes settled again on the obsequious belligerent in front of him, at least that experiment had netted him a nickname.

"Look, I don't care who said it was okay. Nothing gets through without..." A loud klaxon sounded, signaling an immanent pressurization of the bay. Thurston waved his arm sharply at the control room, to no avail. He grabbed a radio from his belt. "There's people on the deck—close it down."

"Voleish," his earbud crackled, "we've got a transport from the Ring scheduled to dock..."

"I don't care if you have Gabriel bringing Christ's knickers on a bleedin' chariot full of slave boys, the door stays shut." The klaxon grudgingly abated. "I want your arse in my office in fifteen minutes." He switched off rather than waiting for a protest. "Now, like I was saying," he returned his attention to the greasy sod who ostensibly captained the sorry heap of a ship sitting on the number four loading dock, "nothing, but nothing—no drugs, no plants, no animals, no bleedin' baskets of grandma's ashes—get through without going through at least an inspection. Right now, I'm gonna throw it into full quarantine without an inspection if you don't shut up and move along. Your rocket-powered apple cart is holding up the line. Get into the airlock so we can move the next ship in."

He led the captain to the airlock, showed him in first, and did a last scan over the dock to make sure it was clear. A woman in blue coveralls and a denim cap stood next to a stack of containers, at the far end of the dock, watching him. He caught her eye and waved her off. She nodded and strode easily to the lock at the other end of the dock.

Thurston stepped into the lock and cycled it shut.

"Now, you," he turned to the captain who was evidently too blind stupid to get on his way and find a sleep locker for the night, "get out of here. You'll be notified when we're done."

The chastened man slunk out the exit.

Goddammit, where the fuck is Walters? Thurston took the three rights into the control room, and then the fourth back into his office. He sat down at his desk, looked up at the door, and bellowed.

"Rison, get your arse in here!"

Rison, the scrawny trainee that was filling in for Walters, and poorly, shuffled through the door. "Voleish, you said fif..."

"I know what I said, you twit. What the hell are you thinking letting a ship in here when there are people on the dock?"

"There's no..."

"No danger? Son, have you looked out through a porthole recently? Had a chance to bounce down a hallway? Has it remotely occurred to you that you're up in the sky like fuckin' Superman?"

"I'm not a moron..."

"You aren't? Rison, you just started a small craft dock cycle on a loading dock on a planet with no atmosphere! You did take biology, didn't you? Occurs to you that men generally breathe air, don't it? Chewing on vacuum at negative twenty five sounded like gettin' a blow job at the lake did it?"

"It's an airlock, Voleish. Air. Lock. Means it ain't likely to leak vacuum. That's kind of the point of the things."

"And I suppose they never fail when you're moving ships that weigh thousands of tonnes around like Barbie dolls? Do you know what it takes to cause a leak? Those doors are sealed with rubber gaskets, my boy. It don't take a sodding lot to make 'em get all squirmy on you."

"They're checked every..."

"And that don' even get into the matter of moving around that much metal on a populated platform. It has dawned on you that the physics involved in a tower of bomb-powered scrap metal giving a friendly shove to a meter and a half of meat and toothpicks means you're gonna be swabbing the fucking deck with bleach to get the stains out?"

"Voleish..."

"Shut your trap. You've lost speech privileges in this room, kiddo. This dock has a book, and we run by it, down to the nearest bloody comma, and if we don't, bad things happen. Very bad things. Things that you'll dream about when you're ninety and wishin' you could get that cute missy at the end of the bar to stop thinkin' of her grandpa when she looked at you. You sat through six months of drilling and training on those procedures before you got your posting here. There is no excuse for that kind of slipshod work. First, you dock the ship on the dolly. Then you give the all clear signal. Once it's answered back, then you check the dock lock status. If all the air doors aren't sealed, you fuckin' seal 'em. Then, and only then, once everyone's inside, and all the doors are closed, then you can cycle the lock.

"Do you get me?"

Rison stood stock still.

"It's okay for you to talk to answer me."

Rison nodded, defiance still spread across his face like liquid shit. "Yeah, I get you."

Bloody teenagers. "Good. You're suspended until you get recertified. You'll get three quarter pay as long as you show up to class. Now, get off my dock and don't come back until you're ready to operate here like an adult."

Rison opened his mouth and closed it again, uselessly trying to remember the English language. He gave up, nodded, and stalked out of the office.

"Somebody gotta kick some sense into that kid." He grumbled as he stood and walked back into the control nest.

"Okay, what've we got?"

"Scheduled transport from the Ring sliding into loading dock C now." Furgeson paged through the tactical displays on his screen. "Got another two staged up."

"Any empty slots the right size for 'em?"

"Yeah, G and J are open."

"Well, boys, lube 'em up an' slide 'em on in. We got cargo to move." Thurston slid his eyes over the bank of monitors and spotted the woman from earlier talking to Rison out in the main corridor. "Well, now, what're you doin' here?" he mumbled to no one in particular

"Furgeson, I gotta check something out. Cover me here."

"Roger, Voleish. Should I buck customs inspection upstairs?"

"Yeah. Don't let anything through without a once-over. I don't want those straight boys up at CID coming down here again and looking up our skirts. Keep the dock as tight as an altar boy, I'll check out any 'exceptions' when I get back. Just set 'em off to the side."

"Will do."

Thurston strolled out of the control room and then broke into a jog. The woman was haunting his dock without a badge—and, badge or no, she should have been cleared through him. He sure as hell wasn't gonna let Rison give her what she was looking for. Was she CID?

The cargo bay halls, white like a hospital, fell past him as he ran to the north access hatch where the bay linked up with the rest of the spaceport.

"There you are." He rounded the last corner just as Rison was disappearing through the hatch into the terminal. She—whoever she was—was making notes on a PPD. Leaned up against the wall like a boy who wasn't quite comfortable in his skin yet. Pity. "Hey!"

She turned and faced him as he bounded to a stop in front of her, then nearly collapsed as the oxygen caught up with his brain. "Jesus! You think I'd been suckin' on the ethylene hoses."

"Are you okay?"

"I'm fine, girly." He took a couple measured breaths, then stood straight again and eyeballed her. "I want to know what you're doing on my dock."

"Ah, you must be Voleish."

"Been talking to Rison?"

"Well, you can't really call it talking. But he did recommend you for the job of antichrist."

"Let me know when the position opens up, will ya? It'll save me from dealin' with damn fool kids like him." He paused for a moment and looked her over. Short, youngish, brown eyebrows trailing to red in the corners. Not the type that CID usually put on snoop jobs—they wanted blokes who could go up toe to toe with the dock rats. Bucking cargo for a living wasn't great for the brain, but it didn't do half bad by a hardbody. "None of that explains who you are and what the hell you're doin' in here without clearance."

"Got somewhere we can talk?"

"Depends. What are we gonna talk about?"

"I'm trying to find one of your boys."

"Look, lady, my boys are my business. Take your questions back to your editor and leave me alone."

"I'm not a reporter, Mr. Shaw. The Green Lady sent me."

"The Green Lady, eh?" He ran the tips of his fingers over the close-cropped beard on his chin. "What's she want here? We pay our dues."

"She's looking for Scott Walters."

"Well, then..." He regarded her again. She played with a stacked deck, this. And he couldn't afford to piss off the Green Lady. He reached down to his belt and picked up his handset. "Furgeson, I'm gonna be a while. Hold it down there."

"Roger that, Voleish."

Thurston replaced the handset and gestured out into the terminal. "This way." He led her out into the broad half-pipe and over to a sofa next to a fountain, still near enough the hatch that he could make it back in an emergency. Furgeson was sharp, he'd call if he got in over his head.

The dock didn't run itself.

"So, since when does the Lady care about what the cargo buckers do with their free time?"

"The lady doesn't reveal her intentions to me. She says jump," she cocked an eyebrow at him in what he supposed was a flirt. He shuddered unpleasantly. "I jump."

"Take an eye-stroll over there toward the passenger terminal." Thurston nodded past her at a dashing thirtysomething porter pushing a cart. Tight arms, broad shoulders, slight moustache, long legs. Delectable.

"Very nice. And...?" She looked back at him, and he made sure she caught him checking the porter out. Her eyes opened wider. "Oh."

"Now we understand each other. Dockrats are the new priesthood."

"I was wondering where you were all hiding."

"Well, where else can you be surrounded by it and not have to worry about accidentally picking up the wrong bloke? It's not the arts, sweetie, we ain't dancers or choir boys. Most of us here second or third generation, the rest were shipped here for one damn thing or another. Ain't got the money or the manner or the temperament to play desk-arse, an' we're exposed to enough radiation by our third year that we're basically infertile, so the pay ain't high enough for family men. Mostly it's just us bachelors."

"Understood. Sorry."

"Skip it. Ask your questions, we don't want to keep the Lady waiting."

"How long did you know him?"

"Walters? He's been on my crew for years. Good man, never missed a day in his life that I didn't send him home for comin' in too off his game..." Thurston stopped. She was reporting to the Lady, she didn't need the gory details. "He was a good 'un. Thorough worker, generous, a real sweet ol' cock. He'd give you his left nut if it'd make the day go better."

"Where'd he go?"

"Fucked if I know. He left me a message, some rubbish about his mum dying out on Nineveh, he'd be back in a few months. Out of nowhere. Thing is, he told me once that his mum had died years back in some accident. Bloody peculiar. I figure the old sod got itchy and wanted out."

"So he just left a message one day and never showed up?" She was scribbling on her PPD like a bleedin' stenographer.

If the Lady finds something, what'll she do to him? Will she send this little wisp of a girl out after him?

"Voleish?"

He focused back on her and inclined his head.

"I suggest," she paused long enough that he knew it was anything but a suggestion, "that you cooperate. I don't have to tell you what happens when the Lady gets piqued."

"I run my dock and don't give much of a fig about anything else."

"You run a dock that almost got caught letting smugglers through last year, and now your second is missing. That's bad, Voleish. Security is the Lady's game, and you're a hole in it."

She had him. Not such a wisp after all. But she wouldn't shut him down. She can't be that stupid. If the Lady is interested, Scott's in trouble. Or is trouble.

"Look, I don't know who the hole is. I run a tight dock up here, nothing gets through without orders from the Lady's Right Hand."

"She's gonna take convincing."

"I keep logs that make a larch look like a bleedin' toothpick, girly, she's welcome to inspect them anytime."

"You have her box number. Drop them in. I'm sure it will help allay her suspicion." Gods below, she's good at this. "So come on, Voleish. Tell me what happened. Why did he leave?"

Thurston sighed. "You promise me you won't let the Lady space him?"

"What makes you think I have that kind of influence?"

"Let me tell you something, Red: The Green Lady ain't no tosser. I hear tell that she killed ten men with a cheese knife when she was only as high as my hip. She took Darkside as her own when she was all of seventeen. She don't lose, and she don't send in a little girl to do an enforcer's job. If she sent you down here, she trusts you, and sure as the secret gospel she tells you a damn sight more than you're lettin' on."

She nodded, smiling slightly. "Go on, then."

"He had a new boy, some kid fresh off the boat. He met him up at One Eyed Jack's place, came in the next morning a smitten kitten. Starry-eyed and couldn't put his mind on the dock.

"I've known Scott since he got his first cert, and I've never seen him in love. He loved that man. Wouldn't stop talking about him. Tyler was all he could talk about. Walters was always in early, but after he met Tyler he was in late every morning, takin' off early every night, always a smile wider than the sky.

"Then he vamoosed. Up and fucking gone overnight. His boy too. Both of 'em, like they was raptured.

"The morning he didn't show up I went up to his flat and banged on the door, but they didn't answer. I figured they couldn't be roused for heaven nor hell, so I went back to the nest. That's where I got the note.

"I tell ya, Red, somethin' bout this stinks." He shook his head, realizing that under his irritation he really was worried about his old flame. "I hope he's okay and that new boy of his hasn't buggered him and left him high and dry."

The girl nodded. "What else can you tell me?"

"That's all I got. You tell that Lady of yours that I don't like you nosin' around my dock and talking to my people. Next time she wants somethin', she can talk to the Right Hand, or if she has to she can talk to me. But this," he leaned forward and thumped the bill of her cap, "cloaked up bullshit don't carry water where I come from. If you all down there want to see your cargo get lost, you just keep interferin' here, or pray that Jesus remembers where he left his hat, because short o'that, you won't break the dockrats open. You don't have the balls."

"I'll carry your message, Mr. Shaw. That'll be all."

He stood up, harrumphed, and looked down at her. This little girl was perhaps the only hope he had of ever seeing Walters again. God was cruel, after all. "You find Scott, you bring him back. You hear me?"

"If we find him, we'll bring him back." She nodded politely at him, dismissing him.

Read the rest of
Predestination: Book 1 of *The Antithesis Progression*
Available in paperback or ebook at www.jdsawyer.net
or wherever books are sold